Something crashed on his skull and everything went black

When he came to he was lying on the floor of the apartment. He looked up to see he was surrounded by grim-looking men. One of them kicked him in the side.

"Leave him alone," he heard a voice say. "We don't want any bruises on him."

He groped for his gun—but it wasn't there.

The voice spoke again; "You've meddled once too often, Simon Kaye. We're going to put you out of action—permanently."

"Hillary Waugh consistently shows professional skills of a hard, glittering kind: his detective stories are among the most intelligent being written in America today."—The Times Literary Supplement.

Hillary Waugh
is also the author
of Raven House Mystery
The Glenna Powers Case

She went looking for help—and she found death.

She was one woman alone facing the ruthless drug dealers who were ruining the town's young people.

She had appealed to investigator Simon Kaye for help. But he hadn't been able to prevent her murder. Racked with guilt, he swore to avenge her. He searched for her killers in the mean streets and greasy bars where the dealers plied their trade.

But there was one thing he didn't realize. Drugs aren't confined to the slums. Heroin can be found in the fanciest mansion in town.

And so can murder!

Hillary
Waugh

THE DORIA RAFE CASE

Raven House edition published August 1982.

Second printing

ISBN 0-373-63043-3

Printed in Canada

IT WAS ONE OF THOSE BLUE MONDAYS, rainy and cold, with March still acting like a lion. I didn't have any cases I liked, and worst of all, Eileen was sick. Eileen's my secretary and she can set you up even when she's down, but her voice over the phone was so runny and snuffly that I told her to stay in bed with rum, lemon juice and honey. She'd have come in if I needed her, but I said no, I'd answer the phone, make the coffee and mind the office instead of tailing people in the rain. She offered to send her cousin to pinch-hit, but I nixed that, too. Her cousin is husband-hungry, and the other time she subbed she wasn't only pushing thirty, she was pushing chicken soup. I didn't have to eat for a week.

By eleven o'clock I'd done all the inside office work I could find and dictated all the letters into a cassette. Eileen hates transcribing from tape. She'd rather do it from her notes. That'll teach her to catch cold.

After that I made what phone calls I could, sent out for a sandwich, then settled down to a gloomy afternoon reading the reception-room magazines and watching the rain bead on the windows. The phone didn't ring, and the only person who came in was an elderly gentleman who mistook me for the watch repair shop down the hall.

That was until quarter of three. Then the outer door opened and a young girl peeked in. She looked nineteen and had the shy air that nineteen-year-olds have. Her hair was black and wavy; her eyes were dark brown, heavy lashed and enormous. Her body was slender and small boned and encased in a dripping white raincoat. She wore clear plastic boots over high heels, carried a white purse, tan umbrella, and had one of those thin plastic head coverings over her hair and under her chin.

She looked first at Eileen's empty desk, then saw me in the inner sanctum, entered uncertainly and closed the door. I rose and went to the entrance. "You looking for me?" I expected that she, like the old gentleman, wanted a watch repaired.

She nodded instead. "You're Simon Kaye."

"That's right."

"You haven't changed at all. I knew you right away."

I stepped aside. "Thanks. And you're . . . ?"

"Doria Rafe. You might remember my folks. They have a store on—"

"Rafe," I said. "Candies, novelties, ice cream, soda pop—name it, they had it."

She nodded shyly.

"And every magazine in the world. Comic books! I used to spend a couple of afternoons a week reading all the comic books, and only buying something when my conscience hurt." I brought her into the office and helped her off with her coat. "How are your folks?"

"All right," she said without a great deal of conviction.

I sat her in the client's chair and leaned against the desk. "Wait a minute," I said. "I remember you. You always had a dirty face and hands, and black knees. But one thumb was white because you sucked it. And you had a green tricycle."

"I remember the tricycle," she said.

"You were about four years old and played in the dirt yard out back." I cocked an eye at her. "Even then, underneath that dirty face, I could tell you'd grow up to be a beauty."

She flushed and looked at her lap. "I only want to be beautiful for one person," she said.

That was a nice, noble attitude, but wasted. She was going to be beautiful to a lot of people. I smiled. "And I gather you already know who the person is?"

She nodded, again shyly, and wouldn't look at me.

"Is that why you're here?"

She shook her head.

"You didn't just come in because it was raining?"

She shook her head again. Then she looked up.

"Lisa Vargas is a friend of mine. I mean, she's much older, but I know her."

"Lisa Vargas?"

"She came to you two years ago. She had a problem. You helped her."

"Yes," I said. "That's right. I remember."

"You were nice to her. She didn't have much money, but she came from the same part of town where you grew up and you were nice to her. You didn't charge her too much."

I could see where this was going. "And you come from the same part of town, you have a problem, and *you* don't have much money."

"No, no," she said, looking up quickly. "I don't have any problem. Well, I mean, I didn't come here to hire you to do anything. I thought maybe, because you're so much older and wiser, and you grew up in the same neighborhood and you knew my family, that you could give me the answer to a question."

"I can try." I looked her over as she sat there, slender, shy and nervous, and I tried to guess what was on her mind, but I couldn't even imagine. "What's the question?"

She took a deep breath and held it all the way through. "Do you think a girl would be doing wrong entering a life of prostitution if it was to earn money for a noble cause?"

That was the last question in the world I expected, not just because of the way she looked, but because of the business I'm in. What would a girl come to a private detective with that kind of question for?

But she was dead serious. She looked at me hopefully and expectantly, as if private detectives were where you naturally went to get right answers to questions like that. You'd want to laugh, except the answer was very important to her and there was nothing funny about why she was asking it.

I didn't even smile. I said to her, "I don't think you've come to the right place to ask that kind of a question. I'm not saying this because I'm trying to duck it, it's just that I'm not equipped to give you an answer. It's not my province." Then I said, "The person you should talk to is Father McGuire. You must know him if you go to church. As a matter of fact, he and I grew up together, so if you remember me you should remember him." I rose from the desk in my dismissive attitude and said, "So I think the person you should go see is Father McGuire. He's the one who can give you—"

Doria didn't rise with me. "I've already seen him," she said.

"And what did he say?"

"Just what I thought he'd say—that it would be wrong no matter how noble the cause."

"Well, then?"

"So I thought I'd ask you what you thought."

"You wanted a second opinion, in other words?"

"Yes. You see, Father McGuire isn't a man of the world the way you are. I don't mean he isn't a fine man and a good priest, but he's led a sheltered life—"

I burst out laughing. "Sheltered? You should've grown up with him."

She flushed. "But I mean—he turned to the holy life and lives. . . well, he doesn't live the way the rest of us do, so he can't really understand why the rest of us feel the way we do. And I thought that you grew up where I did and know people I know and know how people like me might feel and—and—"

"And if you came to me, I might give you the answer you want to hear instead of the one Father McGuire gave you."

She lowered her head. "Well, I thought you might be more—broad-minded, more understanding." She looked up again. "The cause really *is* noble."

"And you believe the end justifies the means?"

"Well, doesn't it? Just because Father McGuire doesn't believe it—"

"It doesn't, Doria, and you're hearing that from a nonchurchgoer."

Her features were starting to crumble. She didn't know whether she was glad or sorry at my answer, whether to weep in despair or sigh with relief, and her face shaped into an expression halfway between.

I said, "Are you going to tell me what this cause is that you want to become a prostitute for?"

"I didn't say I was talking about me," she answered.

"You didn't have to. Come on, what is it?

You're here, so you might as well tell me the whole story."

She thought about that for a bit and decided to go ahead. "Maybe after you hear what I tell you," she announced, "you might change your mind. You might decide I ought to become a prostitute."

"That's right," I said, but I didn't expect her to believe me. "Maybe I might."

She started in. It was about the store her mom and pop had run for lo these many years. For a long time now they'd been paying weekly protection money. She wasn't sure when it had started because she only learned about it recently.

"Protection money?" I said, leaning against the desk again, stroking my chin like some kind of wise man. "I didn't know that."

"You haven't been around the neighborhood much the past ten—fifteen years."

I admitted I hadn't. "But you've only just come to know about it yourself? Why?"

It seemed that the family had managed to pay off the protection collector every week and have enough left over to survive. But about six months ago the demands were suddenly increased, and the family could no longer make ends meet.

I said, "And that's when you first learned about it?"

Doria nodded. "My folks couldn't keep it secret any longer."

"Was there any explanation for the increase?"

She shook her head.

It was a foolish question. That's not the way they do things. All they tell you is ante up or else; they don't give you a sing-along to go with it. "Then what?"

"One week my parents couldn't make the payment. The man came for the money and they couldn't give him all of it."

"And?"

"Two nights later the front of the store got bombed out."

"I see."

Doria bit her lip. "So, now the insurance company won't insure us anymore, so if they bomb us again my folks'll go out of business. But they can't raise the money to meet the payments. And the man who collects from them has told them that if they don't, worse things are going to happen to them than just being bombed." She looked up at me with those great searching brown eyes. "Now do you see?" she asked. "Mom and pop might get killed. They can't possibly meet the payments. So I thought that, well, perhaps I could raise the money. But there's only one way I could do it." Her eyes were searching me again. "I mean—you know."

"Yes," I said. "I know." I stroked my chin some more. It doesn't make me feel wise, but it's supposed to make me look wise, which is almost the same thing. "Have your folks gone to the police about this?"

"Oh," she said, aghast. "They wouldn't dare.

The police couldn't do anything, and besides, they'd be killed."

That shows you how wise I am. Even Doria knew that much. I said, "So you figure the answer is for you to walk the streets?"

Doria said simply, "I don't know what else I can do."

"And what would your family think of that?"

Doria put fingers to her mouth in horror. "Oh, I'd never let them know. I'd die first."

"And what about your boyfriend? What're you going to do about him?"

"He wouldn't know, either," Doria answered softly. "I couldn't stand for him to know that. I'd break off with him. I can find an excuse. I'll make up something so he'll think I hate him." She looked to me. "I'll be able to manage it. I'll manage everything."

She looked as if she could. She was prepared to go the route and she had the inner toughness that would see her through. I said to her, "All right, that's one solution. Is that the only one? Have you thought about alternatives? Don't you have friends, contacts, others who can give you a helping hand?"

"Not really." She shook her head. Her lips tightened and she added a firm, "No."

"What's that mean?" I asked. "What's this other possibility that you're rejecting?"

Her chin stayed firmly set. "It's not a possibility at all."

"I want to hear about it anyway."

A bitter light came into her eyes. "I know someone who might give me the money," she said. "But I wouldn't want to pay the price he'd ask. I'd rather walk the streets."

"Pass it by me a little more slowly, please! Who will give you what for what?"

Doria sighed, but the hate remained in her eyes. "There's a man," she told me, "by the name of Archie Fallon, who's made a lot of money in real estate. He grew up in our neighborhood. Maybe you know him."

Sure, I knew him. I beat him up when I was seven years old and he was fourteen and trying to force himself on a ten-year-old girl. I didn't really beat him up; he was too big to beat up. What I did was bloody his nose and chase him away. I'm not mentioning this to show you what I was at seven, but what he was at fourteen. He was a soft yellow lecher, and I didn't expect twenty-three years would have changed him any. I knew what Doria meant. "I know him," I said.

"Anyway," Doria went on, "Archie has an awful lot of money and he keeps wanting to do things for me—buy me things—take me places. He's been chasing me for a couple of years now. But I won't let him. He wants to go with me. He even wants to marry me, and I know he'd love to pay off my parents' protection money if I'd become his girl." She shuddered at the thought and shook her head. "I'd rather be a prostitute." She said to me, "You can understand that, can't you?"

I said yes, I could.

She wondered if that was a sign. "You mean, then, you think it's all right? I mean about the prostitute business?"

"I didn't say that," I told her.

She chewed her lip. "Then, I don't know what you mean. What should I do?"

"When's the collector coming around?"

"Wednesday. He's coming Wednesday, and we don't have enough money. And if we don't, that means another bomb, or something worse. I'm afraid they'll do something to mom and pop."

She looked ready to erupt into tears, screams or panic, and I said, "All right, all right, just relax and we'll talk about it. Getting excited isn't going to buy a thing." I put my hands on her shoulders, and if the action didn't totally soothe her, it did keep her off the walls. Then I sat in the other customer chair and stretched my legs to show her how easy it was, and told her to tell me everything she could. Who picked up the money, when did he come by, how was it handed over, what kind of bills did they pay him off in, had they ever put up any fuss, did they know who else was being "protected"?

There was a lot Doria didn't know. Mom and pop had always kept it top secret, so she only had the bits and pieces. The collector was new—he'd only come around after the price became exorbitant. He was young and arrogant, quite a departure from the last collector, who'd been middle-aged, plump and unobtrusive. The older collector had come and gone like a landlord collecting the rent. They'd hand him the envelope and he wouldn't open it to count the take. He'd tuck it in his pocket and go on to the next collection point. Sometimes he even said thank-you. You almost didn't mind forking over your dough to someone like him.

No, she didn't know his name.

What about the new guy, the young punk?

He was a different cut of cloth. He'd open the envelope and count every bill, laying them out one by one on the counter, licking his fingers to make the bills slide, writing the totals on the back of the envelope. And he made both mom and pop stand there while he counted, even if a customer was waiting at the register. He was always surly, and he wore a gun on his hip. You could see the special gun belt he wore when he opened his jacket, and you could see the posterior bulge even when his jacket was buttoned. Doria believed it was meant to be seen.

The pickup day was Wednesday, but the time was anywhere from one till five. Doria could not anticipate his arrival, which meant either that the operation was loose or that it was scrambled to throw off heisters. Either way there would be checkpoints all down the line. If Macho Moneyman called in at this collection point and didn't call in at the next one, the higher-ups would have narrowed the search area. That's one of the things to expect in an operation like this.

As for the rest of it, her folks had never put up

a fuss. They didn't have the muscle even to think of such a thing. The money they gave him was what came in over the counter. That meant bunches of old, unidentifiable grubby bills. Macho's little ploy of licking his fingertips to aid his counting was obviously calculated to intimidate, not speed up the action.

There were others on the protection-racket list, of course, but Doria didn't know who they were. She wouldn't even volunteer a guess.

I shook my head. It was par for the course. The average citizen in our country is lame, halt and blind. That's what makes this such a field of clover for the crooks. Give them two good legs plus one good eye and they're three points up on the rest of us.

But that's neither here nor there. Doria had come for help, not sermons. I gave her what I thought was the best solution to the problem: don't pay Macho Man his fee.

Doria got so disturbed at that suggestion I had to calm her down again. This was exactly the situation she was trying to avoid. How could I suggest such a procedure? They'd been bombed once and threatened thereafter. To her way of thinking, the one option not open to them was to default on the payment.

"Why?" I asked, playing the innocent. "What would happen? And don't give me end results. I want you to tell me the steps that would take place."

"Steps?" She was slightly hysterical. "You

want steps? I'll give you steps." She counted on her fingers. "First off, this man—this horrible man—would report to his superiors that Martino and Arissa Rafe had failed to produce the expected money. The superiors, whoever they are, would set the necessary machinery in motion to punish Martino and Arissa Rafe as an example to the rest of the contributors. And since contributions would be important to the superiors, they would make the punishment very severe, so the others would stay in line."

Doria was one damned street-smart kid. For all her big staring eyes and modest mien, she knew we live nearer to hell than to heaven. I nodded and said, "You know the ways of the world, all right. You learned them young."

Doria said simply, "I learned my neighborhood. That's all I know."

I sat up in my chair and put on a little arrogance myself. Sometimes it's what the recipe calls for. "Okay," I said, "you've given me one of the things that might happen if your folks don't give this punk his dough. But there are others."

"What others?"

"I have one I'd like to try."

"Like what?"

Like the rest of the old neighborhood, she was suspicious and had to be shown. And she wasn't interested in just the pattern; she wanted to know the number of stitches to the inch.

I smiled and stood up. "That's something I'd want to talk to your folks about."

She didn't get up with me. "You want to do something," she said accusingly. "You want to get involved."

"Is that bad? You said you needed help."

"I didn't. That's what you said."

"No, I didn't. I said you shouldn't pay this creep. And if you're going to take my advice, I'd better be on hand to make sure you aren't sorry."

"Meaning you want to get paid." She stood up, and I thought she was going to sweep out of the office in royal disdain, but she couldn't really afford the luxury. Instead she gave me her haughtiest chin-up stare. "How much?"

"Five dollars," I said, to say something.

"Five dollars? That's ridiculous. Do you think we're on welfare?"

"How about one half of what's in the envelope, provided the guy doesn't come back again?"

"You think he won't come back again?"

"You're not answering my question."

She shook my hand. "Of course," she said. "And after that," she added, "it's all right with you if I walk the streets?"

That's what I call a vote of confidence.

I GAVE THE OFFICE over to the answering service and took my heap out to the old neighborhood. The neighborhood is a slum in anybody's language; it was the place I couldn't wait to get away from, it was the place I never went back to, and the rain was coming down as if it had to do all of April's showers today. Even so, it beat sitting in the office with no Eileen.

Rafe's storefront looked like a dying relic. I don't mean because plywood sheets replaced the glass show windows the bomb had blown out; it was the weathered sign with the faded letters that a twenty-twenty could just about read from across the street.

Inside, where the bomb damage didn't count, there was the same old look. The magazines were new and bright and they weren't the ones I used to read twenty years ago, but the candy-bar rack was there and the candy was the same, though the bars were smaller and the prices bigger. It was the showcases. Some of the novelties on display behind the grimy glass hadn't been changed since my day. They weren't novelties; they'd died of old age and I was looking at mummies.

Mr. and Mrs. Rafe were behind the counters, dishing out sodas and ice-cream cones to the newest crop of youngsters, selling papers, tobacco and knickknacks to fleeting adults, ignoring the two or three kids who devoured the comic books by the magazine stand as I had once devoured their comic books. It was an aspect of my life that hadn't changed, which meant that, except for being grayer now, they hadn't changed. I'd left them and their store in my past, as the little kids sitting rapt in the comic books would tomorrow leave them in their past, but for Mom and Pop Rafe, the store was their past, present and future, and they would die there. That fact, when I entered their dingy little place, bothered me, but they didn't seem to mind.

The funny thing is, they remembered me—not my name, but my person. Mrs. Rafe said, "You always sat on that corner of the rack where that blond boy's sitting. And you'd spread a comic book across your knees and chew a Milky Way, and you'd go through three comic books for every Milky Way."

She knew me well. I said, "How could you make any money out of my sating myself on your comic books?"

"Oh," she said, "you'd be surprised what young boys reading comic books can do to make a store inviting to the people who do the real purchasing. And," she added, pinching my cheek, "you spent all the money in your pockets on Milky Ways."

I hadn't really known Mrs. Rafe before. She and her husband were those grown-ups who controlled our oasis in the slum. You didn't know if they were benevolent or cruel; all you knew was that they were grown-ups and they were in control. So you read the comic books always with the finger of fear in your stomach lest the grown-ups should tell you to put them back or pay for them. The Milky Way bars were altar sacrifices to appease their unknown but feared appetites. (If you bought something significant—like a candy bar instead of a few chocolate kisses—maybe they wouldn't notice you desecrating their comic-book stand and reading free.)

They could handle that, all right. They were wise heads and they couldn't say no to children. Give them their little shop and they could make a living. They wouldn't graduate from there, as the rest of us would, but they didn't want to. Like teachers in a school, they were content to feed the needs of an ever changing population of children and adults.

Now, however, the scene was changing. Now they were facing problems beyond their scope. The store they could manage; the demands of the extortionists, they could not.

I got Papa Rafe out in the back room and put it to him. I didn't say what Doria had in mind as a fund raiser, but I let him know she'd told me the score and I'd been hired to help.

"Hired?" he said, looking at me as something other than a benignly neglected comic-book reader. "I never hired you."

"That's right," I said and told him *she* had. I went on for a bit with the details to make sure he understood I knew all the secrets and he didn't have to play dumb.

He walked around the room for a bit, looking as if he'd swallowed a bat. Martino was proud, like anybody worth his salt, and he didn't want to lean on others. This time, though, he didn't have much choice.

"What's Doria going to you for?" he complained. "I never gave her the right."

I wasn't going to get onto that subject. I said, "I'll tell you, padre, I don't even know what I'm doing here. You're in a tunnel and the train's coming after you, but they forgot to open the other end and you're up against the wall. There's no way out, except that your daughter thinks I might be able to save you. Your daughter's very nice and very beautiful, but she's not very bright. You understand?"

"No."

"You make it easy, padre. All I have to do is say goodbye and go home. And believe me, there's nothing I'd like better. But your daughter wants me to do something about the trouble you're in. She thinks I can help you."

"My daughter is an idiot."

"You don't need help?"

"She doesn't know what I need."

The old man sank into a chair at a table and leaned his head in a hand. Something inside was telling me to get out of there, that it was a losing proposition all around. There was no money in it;

there was no solution, no easy end. When the ants crash your picnic, what good does it do to stomp on some?

If I were smart I'd pat the old man on the shoulder, wave goodbye to Doria and hightail it back home to my condominium, pour myself a highball and light a candle or blow a kiss or do whatever would propitiate Mother Nature and get Eileen over her sniffles by morning.

But Papa Rafe was bowed and shrunken. You look at him and see the end of the road. It's not today or tomorrow, but it's close, and you don't want to bring it closer. Let time move the days.

I said, "Who's this creep who's bleeding you?"

That opened his eyes. He answered hoarsely, "How much did she tell you?"

"Everything she knew, but it's not enough. Tell me about the creep who comes for your protection money."

He didn't confide easily. We went around the mulberry bush a couple of times before it came out. When he told it to me, it was in hushed whispers and only because he'd known me as a kid and I wasn't connected with the FBI, the official police or any harmful organization. Also, though I was beyond the pale as far as the Church was concerned, Father McGuire didn't regard me as a lost soul, so I must be on the side of God.

I said that if God took sides, I certainly tried to be, and asked again about the collector.

Martino almost wept. The collector was a very

young man, he told me. But he was so hard and harsh. Did I know the movies about the Nazis and the Jews and the concentration camps? Martino understood those movies. He felt like the Jew; and the young collector, he looked like the Nazi.

"Who else pays him money besides you?"

Martino didn't know. It wasn't the kind of question a Jew asked the head of the concentration camp.

"How much do you pay?"

The figure he gave me was far beyond what a reasonable extortionist could expect to collect on a weekly basis. It sounded as if the boss man was a greedy feather plucker determined to kill the goose that laid the golden eggs.

"And he collects on Wednesdays?"

Martino nodded.

"Do you have enough to pay him?"

Martino didn't skirt the question. "If I can take out a loan."

"But the chances aren't good?"

He shook his head. "Not since the bomb."

"How much without a loan?"

He sighed. "I can't give him more than all I've got."

"All right," I said, and decided I had holes in my head. "I'll tell you what we'll do. I'll be your new helper in the store—"

"I can't hire a helper. I don't need a helper."

"Maybe you can't hire a helper, but you sure as hell need one. You need someone to help you pay off this creep. What's the creep's name, by the way?"

Martino shuddered and looked around. He feared having the man who terrorized him referred to as a "creep" in his presence. Finally he swallowed and said that he did not know the collector's name.

"What about identification?"

He didn't know that, either.

Then how did Martino know he was the man you paid the protection to?

Because the former collector had brought him around one day and said that thereafter Martino would give the money to the new man.

I queried him further, but that was all Martino knew.

I looked at the man sitting at the table, bruised, bent, all but broken, and I had—one last time—that flitting feeling that I should get the hell out of there and head for the hills. You can't solve the problems of the world. You can't right the wrongs, adjust the injustices, heal the sick, feed the poor, end the crime.

On the other hand, you can't turn your back. You can't walk out on the world and alibi yourself with quaint phrases like, "What can I do?" or, "This, too, shall pass!" Well, I don't mean *you* can't, or *they* can't, or *someone else* can't; I mean *I* can't.

I said, "All right, padre, I'm going to try to do something."

"I'm not a padre."

"It's a nickname, all right? I talk in screwy ways, all right? What I'm saying is, I'm going to come here on Wednesday and you're going to give me the envelope with the money in it. And it's only going to be what you used to pay, before somebody up the line decided to treble it."

Martino swallowed. "He won't like it."

"What he likes and dislikes doesn't matter. What matters is what we do about him. So on Wednesday I'm going to be your employee in charge of payoffs; which means that when he comes in for the money, you send him to see me."

"He won't like that," Martino said nervously. "He always makes me pay him in person."

"That's all right, Martino," I told him. "We're going to change the rules."

I gave him my hearty smile, the one that says, "It's in the bag!" and got up.

"Your fee?" Martino said, struggling to his own feet. "What is your fee?"

"For the present, as I told your daughter, one half of what I save you."

"Hah," Martino said without mirth. "That will be nothing."

"Then you lose nothing."

MONDAY NIGHT is when Father McGuire and I have a more or less standing chess game. If you don't know, Jack and I grew up together and we've been battling over a chessboard ever since we learned the game in ninth grade. Usually we play at his place on the grounds that if I go there, it looks to the observer as if I am seeking God, whereas if Jack comes to my place, it looks as if I *need* God. That's not the kind of rumor I'd like to see get around.

Anyway, between moves I brought him up to date on the Doria Rafe business, found out what she'd told him, and revealed what she'd told me.

When I said that Archie Fallon was Doria's alternative to walking the streets, he made a face.

"Archie Fallon?" he said. "If she'd told me about Archie, I would have understood her dilemma better."

"Don't tell me if you'd discovered he was the alternative, you'd have urged her to walk the streets."

He laughed. "You don't get into heaven with

thoughts like that. No. Nothing justifies that sort of occupation, and you know that as well as I do, no matter how antireligious you claim to be. I mean, instead, I would have better understood the real depths of her problem.'' He shook his head. ''Archie,'' he said, ''is one of those of God's creatures who really put us to the test. Jesus tells us we should love one another, but for me to love Archie, or even to understand why I should, is beyond me. Intellectually I can accept Christ's admonition. Emotionally I cannot manage it.''

''Aren't the Archie Fallons of the world enough to shake your faith in God? How can this loving being you worship create such unlovable monsters?''

''On the contrary, Simon. It renews my awe at the glory of God. It makes me realize how far I have to go and how much I have to grow before I can understand His will, much less carry it out.''

I moved a piece. ''So while you've been contemplating God instead of the chessboard, check. And granting that Archie Fallon is Doria's alternative to streetwalking, what would you have advised her?''

Jack interposed his knight to block the check. ''Don't give me a lady-or-the-tiger problem,'' he said. ''Life is seldom either-or. Usually there are further alternatives.'' He gave me a wise grin. ''And if I know you, you've come up with one. Otherwise you wouldn't be trying to box me in a corner.''

I took his queen rook pawn with my queen. "Check. I'm only trying to box you in a corner to see where you'll jump. You're too smart to get pinned, so you may come up with an escape route I haven't thought of."

"I don't suppose the police would be of much help."

"You grew up in the area. You know the answer to that as well as I do."

Jack pondered the chessboard for a bit. Then he moved his king. "And you say she came to you after she came to me? I don't know what this world is coming to, Simon."

"I think maybe she believes if the meek are going to inherit, they'd better stop being meek."

"And what kind of advice did you have for her? I'm sure it wasn't one of the alternatives you've given me."

"I said she should let me handle it."

Jack arched an eyebrow. "Well, that's an alternative I wouldn't have come up with. I don't think it would have occurred to me to say to her, 'Don't do anything. Let Simon Kaye handle it.'" He smiled. "What are you planning to do?"

I advanced the king rook pawn. "I'm launching another attack on your king."

"You know what I'm talking about."

"I'm going to handle the payoff. Or mishandle it."

Jack shook his head. "I wouldn't if I were you."

"I'm not telling you this so you can say to me,

'Don't.' I'm telling it to you for another reason."

"Which is?"

"If something happens—I mean, if I don't show up for our next chess game or don't answer the telephone or something like that—the reason will have to do with the protection agency that's squeezing Martino Rafe to death."

Jack concentrated his gaze on the chessboard. "My advice to people," he said slowly, "is always, get involved. Do things, be somebody. Don't turn your back on your fellowman. Care for him. It's the only cure for loneliness. But to you I'm saying just the opposite. I'm saying, don't get involved."

"Thanks and all that, but I didn't come to you for advice. I only wanted to let you know where to start looking if I should disappear."

EILEEN CAME BACK TO WORK on Wednesday. She had a slight croak in her voice but otherwise was up to snuff, meaning she was curvaceous, saucy, show-offy, sexy, yet somehow shy. You have to know that girl. She'd bought a new dress that, she said, was to make her feel good, and the V in the front was so low she made all the men feel good.

I didn't see much of her because she had a lot of backlog to get through, and the typewriter chattered constantly. That was fine with me, for I had a lot of work myself and that new dress raised hell with one's concentration. She brought me coffee at ten and stuck her head in the door at twelve to say she'd only take a half-hour lunch break because she didn't want to stay overtime on account of she wasn't fully recovered.

I'd planned to leave while she was out, but now she'd be on hand and want an explanation. It was bad enough telling Father Jack I was going to lay my head on a chopping block without telling it to Eileen. I decided the best tactic would be to give her the address and phone number of the store and tell her to phone me there at quitting time if I hadn't called in. If I wasn't there, she should call Father Jack.

It didn't quite come out that way, though. She returned from lunch and started typing again. Then there was silence. Then she came into my office holding a paper. "What is this thing?" she said, dangling it by thumb and finger as if it were a breeder reactor. "Are you moving?"

It was a rent receipt I didn't expect her to spot in the files, at least not right away. "No."

"This is dated yesterday. Are you going into real estate?"

"It's business, that's all."

She looked at me without any sympathy and understanding at all. "It's business I don't know anything about."

"It only happened yesterday. You were sick."

"I'm not sick now and I still don't know anything about it."

"I need a place to store a few things."

"What sort of things?"

"Private things."

"Female private things? Girl things? Girls? A girl?" She looked as if she thought she knew me better than that, but suddenly wasn't sure. Men don't usually pay the rent on pads unless a woman is going to occupy the pad; but I didn't look old enough or married enough to play that kind of game.

"To tell the truth," I said, "I rented it in hopes you might come there and spend a wild weekend with me sometime."

"Now," she said, looking very grim, "I *know* you're into something you shouldn't be into."

"Ah, me," I said. "Do you give all men the back of your hand like that when they try to show you a good time?"

Eileen isn't very distractable and she's extremely hard to con. "It's dangerous, isn't it?" she said. "This is one of your dangerous jobs again, isn't it?"

"Oh," I said, "I don't think there's going to be any danger at all."

"Where is this place?"

"It's out in the country somewhere. You don't have to worry. Jack McGuire has the address."

"If Father McGuire's in on it, then I know it's dangerous. You don't have anything to do with God unless you're in real trouble."

"Father McGuire isn't God," I reminded her. "He's not even an archbishop."

"All right," she said. "*Don't* tell me about it. But what am I supposed to do when you don't come back?"

"*If*," I said, correcting her phraseology, "I don't come back by five o'clock, you are to call Father McGuire."

"I see," she said tightly. "All I can say is, it doesn't pay to get sick around here. I may find I'm out of a job."

4

I GOT TO THE STORE at ten after one, and old Martino was as nervous as a tightrope walker with the hiccups. He was afraid of the collector's response and wondered if it wasn't a mistake, my making the payment. I said the envelope was short half of the money and what did he think the collector would do to him if I wasn't there?

"What do you think he'll do to *you*?"

"He won't do anything to me," I said. "It's not my money."

Martino didn't comprehend, but he wasn't supposed to. I just wanted him to relax and pretend the guy was coming tomorrow. I persuaded him to get back behind the counter and to give me the high sign when the collector arrived, though I was sure I wouldn't need to be cued. Collectors don't walk into a store like buyers. They walk in like owners.

Mrs. Rafe came down from their home above the store, and that made things better. With someone beside him he could cope. They both could.

So they handled the customers and I sat at the

soda table by the magazine rack and read magazines the way I had as a kid, except that I didn't munch Milky Ways and it wasn't as much fun.

The creep usually came in around three. At least, that was what they told me. But it got to be three-thirty and I hadn't received any high signs and nobody'd asked for the envelope I was carrying in my inside jacket pocket. Meanwhile I was getting a lot of reading done, but not as much as it looked. That's because I only had one eye on the print. The other was on the people flow, in and out, in and out. The customers were frequent but not many. Not more than once or twice were there three wanting to pay for a purchase at the same time. In between there would be dead periods when only the Rafes and I were in the store. Doria, I was told, was taking art courses at the local college, which was why she wasn't around. I sensed mom and pop didn't want her around on payday, anyway.

Then the door opened and in came this kid. He was about five-nine, swarthy, with marcelled black hair and the kind of thin face and concave physique that fitted the "before" figure in the muscle-development ads. He might not have looked prepossessing physically, but that's not really where it's at in this world. It's attitude that counts, and his was right out of Hitler's notebook. He had eyes you couldn't quite call "steely." "Cast iron" was closer to it. He had the tight lip, the strutting stride, the air that comes from power. As I say, he was a punk, so when a punk makes an entrance like the ruler of the universe, you know he's front man for a very hefty backer. He came into the store with the certain knowledge that no one could hurt him. He also had the attitude that cowards love: the feeling that he could hurt at will.

Needless to relate, I didn't have to be told this was our man, but Martino gave me the high sign anyway. There were two customers in the store—the busiest they'd been in the past half hour—and from the way Creepy Boy made his play, I got the feeling he'd been waiting outside for an aeon or two just so he could put on his act in front of an audience.

So now in he strode, directly up to where Martino was fixing a soft drink for a guy on one of the counter stools. He snapped his fingers and moved to the cigar counter as if Martino was supposed to stop serving the customer and come right over. Little creep didn't happen to notice me. I was so busy poring over the magazines, he probably thought I was furniture. I arched an eyebrow at Martino. He gave a slight nod and slopped the drink he was preparing.

The creep didn't notice. He was so impressed with his own importance he'd never learned to observe, to prepare, to guard against the unexpected. He assumed the big shots he worked for took care of all those things.

He leaned on the cigar counter and tapped the glass irritably with a coin. Martino was wiping the spill and putting the glass on the counter for the customer. The customer was turning to look at the ill-behaved young kid who was butting into his purchase.

I got up and went over, moving in on the near side of the kid, between him and the customer. I said, "You looking for something?"

That was a ploy to throw him off balance. His type is never prepared for variations on the theme.

He turned his cold eyes on me. "Do I know you?"

"Not yet, but you will."

He didn't quite know what that meant, and he didn't have a great deal of curiosity. "Get lost," he said, and turned to Martino. "Hey, snot nose," he said peremptorily, trying to reestablish his pattern, "get over here."

I took the envelope out of my pocket and gave him a peek. "Is this what you're looking for?"

He looked at it and at me. The envelope, he recognized. Me, he did not. "Who the hell are you?" he said, paying attention now, deciding to get his bearings.

"I represent Mr. Rafe," I said. "I handle his business dealings."

He looked me up and down one more time and then spit in my face. "I do my business with Martino," he said. "Hey, you guinea wop, get over here! Fast!"

Nobody had ever spit in my face before, and I have to tell you I never knew till then how hard it is to maintain self-control under such circumstances.

I'm proud of myself. I didn't lay the guy out with a lily in his palm as I wanted to. Instead I put a friendly hand on his shoulder and then clamped on the nerve there—you have to know where it is and how to apply the pressure. It's very effective. It didn't make him scream, but he did turn white and buckle.

I eased the pressure so he didn't go to his knees, but my fingers let him know I'd bring him to the floor if he got balky.

"Let's you and me talk about things in the back room," I said to him in a low but cheerful tone. The customer with the soft drink was eyeing us uneasily, but at least he wasn't frightened. Martino was eyeing us, too, and so was his wife. I can tell you, though, *they* were frightened.

As for Sonny Boy, I walked him out into the storeroom, keeping enough pressure on him to make him honest, but not so much he couldn't function.

Out there I closed the door to the store proper and turned him around. "You're a cute kid, sonny," I said, and then I hauled off and belted him one.

He went against the stock shelves and tumbled a lot of stuff down around him when he fell—containers of this and that, mostly unbreakable. As for him, I hit him harder than I meant—there's something about being spit on that brings out the adrenaline—and he lay flat with the whites of his eyes showing below his lids.

Actually, I'd only meant to cuff him around, bloody his nose, black his eyes, crack a few of his ribs. This way I had to hope I hadn't fractured his jaw. I didn't want to lose him to a hospital. But he lay there on his back with blood leaking out of his mouth, and I got worried. I knelt down and ran my fingers along his jawline—but not, of course, until I'd frisked him.

He was an interesting case, a regular walking armament factory. He had a snub-nosed revolver on his hip, a knife around an ankle, a switchblade in one pocket and brass knuckles in another. The inside jacket pocket contained two envelopes like the one Martino had given me—full of money. The only standard equipment he carried was a handkerchief, a wallet and a fistful of change. The handkerchief was initialed with a *Z* and smelled of Brut. The wallet contained more bills than I wanted to count at the moment, but the name-and-address card in the little window was blank.

I let him keep the change. The rest of the stuff went into an empty carton I plucked from the trash barrel. Then I rolled him over, handcuffed him from the rear and rolled him back. I filled a paper cup from the cooler inside the door and threw the water in his face. He stirred, but that was all. I got another cupful and repeated the process. This time he shook his head and his eyes came unshut. He looked blankly at walls and shelves.

I threw a third cup of water at him and he sputtered. He saw me this time all right, and the hate in his eyes would have felt like a red-hot poker if he could've reached me with it, but I keep my drawbridge up around punks.

"Well," I said, "have a nice nap?"

He was just about to mutter some very uncomplimentary words when he discovered he couldn't move his hands, and that stopped him. He jerked and rattled the cuffs enough to discover what was holding him, and then he said, "You're gonna be sorry."

"Not half as sorry as you're going to be, sonny."

He was about to answer that when a hint of thought passed behind his eyes. It was coming through to him that he didn't have his legions lined up outside, that I didn't crumble under his threats, and that at present I had the upper hand. That meant my statement could just possibly be right. He worked his mouth and in the intervening silence pondered his next move.

He didn't have any, and I didn't waste time. I yanked him to his feet and rammed him against the shelves to let him know who was running this particular scene. With his hands behind him and his face exposed, he was at everyone's mercy. He tried not to cringe, but he wasn't cut from hero's cloth. He was as white as his monogrammed handkerchief, only he didn't smell as good. He stunk of fear.

I gave him one small slap across the chops, and it started his mouth bleeding. I didn't mean to bang him like that. It slipped out, I guess. "All right, sonny," I said, when his eyes unglazed,

"I'm going to give you the game plan. I've got a car out back. You're going to ride in the trunk and you're going to ride in it nice and quiet, or I'll hit you with the tire iron. Now I'll tell you something. I hope you'll give me trouble, because I'm itching to crack your skull. *You* won't like it, but it'll make my day. So if you're smart, don't tempt me. Any questions before we go?"

He was white, but he was perspiring. "Where're ya taking me?"

I whacked him in the chops again. "Smart ass. I asked you if you had any questions! Do you understand what you're supposed to do? Do you have it clear?"

He nodded, and the sweat was beading. "Yeah."

I whacked him again. "'Yes, sir.' You got it? 'Yes, sir.'"

There were tears in his eyes. Somebody had taken his toys away. "Yes, sir."

"That's good." I clapped him on the arm. "You learn fast. I think you're going to be my star pupil." I picked up the carton, opened the door to make sure the yard was empty, then shoved him out into it.

5

I DROVE OUT to the house I'd rented, the one Eileen found the receipt for in the file. I'd picked it up for just this purpose, and it had the trimmings I wanted. It was small, isolated, run-down; a place that was off a dirt road, through a broken gate, down a rutted path with grass between the wheel marks. It was a shanty-type homestead sided with imitation-brick sheeting broken by pine-framed windows and a peeling green door. There was a stovepipe chimney and broken chicken wire framing a dirt patch that had been the backyard. There was a rotting hen coop at the far end, for the dirt yard had once been chicken heaven. The chickens were long gone and even the smell had passed, but when you stepped through the broken wire and crossed their happy hunting ground, you knew their ghosts were still there, scratching, clawing, pecking and squawking.

I'd told the agent I wanted a simple place—nothing to live in, mind you, just an escape hatch, a place where I could hide from the alimony lawyer. I peddled that line not because I had an alimony lawyer after me, but because *he* did. It made the right impression and gave him some ideas as to what he could do with the place once my one month's lease ran out.

It was just after four o'clock when I drove into the yard, got out and opened the trunk. Sonny Boy was curled up in a fetal position with his cheek pressed against the mat. He'd been crying.

I closed him in again while I took the carton with his belongings inside the house and set it on the hearth. The house was scantily furnished, the pine floors dusty, the window shades down. There was electricity, there was a fridge, there was water. I turned on lights, went back to the car and heaved Sonny Boy onto his feet. The day was cloudy and there was a nip in the air. The surrounding woods were bleak and still. The house looked like a last outpost, the blending of civilization with wilderness, some kind of remnant that said mankind existed, that Kilroy had been there.

Sonny Boy looked at the house with a kind of despair. All that bravado, all that machismo, that pleasure he got from kicking cripples, was gone. He looked ten years old, and as I said, he'd been crying. You'd feel sorry for him except it wasn't repentance that had seized his soul, it was fear. The forlorn house wasn't telling him to mend his ways, it was only telling him help was far away.

I gave him a boot and shoved him along. He was one of those who only spoke the language of the sword, so you had to draw blood to communicate. We went inside where there was nothing but walls and floors and overhead lights. I told him to sit by the windows, and he gave me no argument. I knelt beside the fireplace and the carton of his belongings.

One by one I held up items. "Nice," I said, showing him the ankle knife, and he winced. He'd hoped he was still wearing it.

"And look at this!" I gave him a glom at the switchblade and tossed it back. "And this." I fitted his brass knuckles on my right hand and made a fist. I looked at it and his jaw. "I never hit anybody with these," I said, "but I've always wanted to try. How are they? Can you really hurt a guy?"

He swallowed and didn't answer.

"Tell me about it," I encouraged. "What's it like? Can you hear the bones crack? Do they draw blood—or is all the damage internal?"

His mouth twitched, and the sweat came out on his face again. He was sure I was going to beat an answer out of him.

I didn't. I changed the subject, but I kept the brass knuckles on my fingers and flexed them periodically. "We can find that out later," I said, and showed him his gun.

"Yes," I said, turning it over for examination. "A nice little instrument. Loaded, too." I pointed it at him idly, and he flinched. "You fire it often?"

He didn't respond, and I aimed it a little to one side and pulled the trigger. There was an explosion, and a black hole appeared in the wall a foot to his left. I thought he was going to faint.

"It works," I said, and examined it some more. "I fired it even with brass knuckles on." I looked impressed. "This is a very nice gun. You must be proud of it." I looked up at him. "What's your name?"

He was so shaken he just stared at me. "Huh?"

I waved the gun impatiently. "What's your name?"

He swallowed, giving himself one last desperate moment to assess his situation. But he didn't know his situation. He didn't know where he was, who I was, where his friends were or even if he had any friends. In the protection racket there aren't any friends. There is only money.

"Your name!"

He tried to think of a dodge, of trusting his backers, of going down with the ship or of saving his skin. It was all there on his face, like reading the news.

He started by giving me as little as he could. "Richie," he said, with an attempt at reluctant sullenness. "You can call me Richie."

"Richie what?"

Again he tried to assess his options. The trouble was, he didn't have the intellect. "Uh, Brown," he told me.

I fired a shot into the wall six inches from his ear. "You know something?" I said. "This is a very loud gun you've got, but nobody in the world can hear it go off." I playfully aimed the gun between his eyes. "What was that last name again?"

"Zullo," he said quickly, and it sounded more likely.

"Well, we'll see if it is," I said. "I hope you're not lying." I reached into the carton again for the money-filled envelopes.

"Listen," he said, even as I put the gun away, "I'm not lying. That's the God's truth! I swear it!"

"Richie Zullo," I said. "That's a nice name. I think I can remember that." I showed him one of the envelopes. "Who gave you this?"

He didn't know. One envelope was like another, and there were no names. All he did was go around once a week and collect envelopes.

"No kidding. Who do you collect envelopes from?"

"I dunno," he said sulkily.

I held up the hand with the brass knuckles on it and did the ominous finger flexing again. "You're going to tell me before I go, Richie boy. You can make it as painful for yourself as you want, but you're going to tell me." I got to my feet. "How much do you want to hurt?"

Brave men will die on the rack before they'll squeal, but cowards will spill their guts before they get a scratch. Richie wet his pants.

"I didn't mean that," he shrieked. "I know where I got 'em. I just don't know the names. Honest, I don't know their names. But I know the people!"

"You called Martino by *his* name, and you called him a 'guinea wop.' "

"But I don't know his last name," Zullo protested. "All I know is he's Martino."

"And the others?" I sat down again, got out a pad and pencil. "Let's have it all, Richie. I want to know who you collect from and how much. I want to know who you pay the money to, where and when. I want to know your cut. I want the whole story. Do you get what I'm saying?"

Richie's tolerance was low. His backers had made sure he knew they were tough, but they didn't tell him they were dedicated. They spelled out the punishment for waywardness but never promised rewards for loyalty.

It works most of the time, but when a member gets into Richie's spot, where the punishment for betrayal is distant and vague, and the punishment for loyalty is violent and now, there's only one way the Richies in this world can go. Salvation says, betray and pray.

He was collecting from four people, he told me. Martino was third on the list, the first two being a delicatessen up the block and Manny's Shoe Emporium three doors away. The fourth was the Vintner Bottle Shop next to the tailor's in the next block. The amount each shopkeeper pitched in varied, but it was the same each week.

Except for Martino. The Rafes' protection fee had suddenly doubled about the time he started collecting and had gone up another fifty percent three weeks later.

"How come?" I asked. "Who's got it in for the Rafes?"

"I don't know," he said. "They upped the price and told me to collect. They didn't tell me why."

"Who's *they*?"

He shook his head. "I dunno who runs the rackets. I only do what I'm told. I keep my nose clean. I'm a nothing. I ain't kidding—sir. They don't tell me what they want, they just tell me what to do."

"And they told you to double up on the Rafe collection?"

He shook his head again, strongly. "No, sir. They only told me how much was supposed to be in each envelope each time and told me to make sure, because I was responsible. I had to turn over so much dough. I didn't even take my cut out. They counted the dough after me and gave me my cut. After they made sure it was all there."

I asked him the rest of the relevant questions, and he gave me the answers without my having to beat him up at all. He didn't take kindly to pain.

The story was that he was breaking in. These four collections were his first responsibilities, the low rung on the ladder. He was collecting for a guy named Louie (the Greek) Bustoni. It was Louie's territory and Louie was letting Richie handle four of his accounts, testing him out, seeing how he would do.

"How many people does Louie collect from?"

"I don't know. Honest, mister—sir. I swear, I don't know. All I know is these four."

"Where do I get hold of this Louie Bustoni?"

Richie Zullo bit his lip. Tears were close to the surface. He didn't want to tell me that. He begged me not to make him. Louie wouldn't like it if I gave Louie a bad time and he learned that Richie had tipped me off.

I nodded very solemnly and took his switchblade out of the cardboard box. "I guess I've got a ways to go," I said. "You're more scared of him than you are of me. You think I'm tenderhearted and he's tough. I'm going to have to change your mind."

A roll of new clothesline I'd bought for the occasion was also in the box. I brought that out, unwrapped it and tied Richie's feet. It was funny the way he twisted and turned but refused to struggle. He didn't want me to do it, but he knew if he put up a squawk, I'd hit him with that tire iron and do it anyway.

I drew his feet up and put a loop around his neck so that if he started to kick he'd choke to death. Then I ripped open his pants and pulled them down, got out the ugly switchblade and nicked his thigh to test the blade. Dark blood welled slowly. He kept that knife razor-sharp.

We can leave it there. I won't tell you what I said I was going to do to him and what I started to do, but I will say that before I drew any more blood, he told me everything I wanted to know.

In fact, there wasn't anything he wouldn't tell me. I got out a pad and pencil, but he talked so fast I couldn't get half of it down. He wanted to tell me about every dream he'd ever had, every girl he'd ever laid, the names and addresses of everyone who'd ever corrupted him in any way. It was one helluva job focusing him on the things that mattered—whom did he pay off to, how much, where, who got him into all this, who was on the take, who was on the make?

Of course, this was pouring out of him like Niagara Falls, and some of the details would have to be checked, but he sure was a fount of information that late Wednesday afternoon.

You learn a lot about people in this business. He was so grateful when I put away the switchblade without castrating him that he would willingly have kissed me in places I don't want to be kissed. I was his friend for life because I hadn't done to him what I'd threatened to do.

Richie Zullo was one of those eager guys who are short of feelings, short of sight and short of time. They sell their souls to endure, but they aren't long for the game.

I MADE A RUN back to the store, and all was calm. Louie Bustoni hadn't been around looking for his bagman, nobody else had given the place a fish stare, and all was as serene and happy as a sated feline.

Doria said, "Did you do it, Simon? I mean, is everything all right now?"

"Not yet, but soon," I said, sounding as much like God as I could. I liked the light in her eyes when she thought about her boyfriend much better than the look she got when she thought about Archie Fallon.

"But there's one thing," I said to her and to them all. "Anything you hear, anything that happens, and I'm not around, you're to call this number. This is my secretary, and she'll process all the information and take all the messages. She's the clearinghouse, you understand?"

I wrote it down for them, then called Eileen on the phone in the back room to tell her what she might be hearing and that she was to have the answering service transfer all after-hours calls to her home. That, of course, made her feel great.

"What the hell are you doing," she said, "trying to set my heart on fire?"

"I beg your pardon?"

"Heart! Heart! You know, the thing that goes pitty-pat—except around you it goes garrumph, garrumph, garrumph. I'm a very young, tender child. I don't need ulcers."

"If they're like the rest of you, I'll bet they'd be beautiful."

"I'll send you framed copies. What are you doing, anyway—trying to make a widow out of me?"

"Widow? Aren't you jumping the gun? We aren't married, that I know of."

"I'm married to my job. That's you, isn't it, God help me?"

"Look," I assured her, "it'll all be over very quickly. Also very painlessly. Maybe by tomorrow morning."

"Meanwhile I'm collecting signatures—"

"Messages!"

"Signatures," she repeated. "Like for a wake." She said sternly, "Listen, Jack Armstrong, I've got just one question. How much are you getting paid for this caper?"

"Always thinking about money," I said.

"Just as I thought," she said. "Not a nickel, right? You're doing this to boost your ego or make the world safe for democracy or some other damned-fool thing, aren't you?"

I got sharp with her, which I almost never do. "Listen," I said, "I don't have time. I've got a schedule to keep. You know that house I rented? If you don't hear from me by tomorrow morning, give the police the address. You got it?"

"I got it," she said brokenly. "What time tomorrow morning?"

"Make it ten o'clock."

"Ten o'clock. Call the police. Where do I send the flowers?"

"You'll hear from me before that."

"Sure I will. Is that all I get to go on?"

"It's all I know myself. Goodbye. I've got to hit the road."

"I could cry. Drive carefully, you damned fool."

"Sure," I said. "And if I'm not back by Saturday, pay yourself your salary. You can sign the checks."

"Oh, shut up."

I took off then and drove the heap to the Belmore Vista, a high-rise complex in a part of town where the apartments have rooms not only for children but for the children's governesses. Except that you don't see any children: they're off raising kids of their own by the time their parents can afford the rent. It's a quiet place with glass walls and a fountain in the lobby, swank but not elegant.

This was where Louie the Greek lived—so Richie told me—but it wasn't where Richie gave him the envelopes. The dough got passed in a deserted spot behind a shed on one of the abandoned piers at the other end of town. Richie's job was to be there at quarter past six every Wednesday evening. Somewhere between then and six forty-five, Louie would show, Richie would hand him the money and Louie would count it and give Richie two new ten-dollar bills for his trouble. The envelopes contained over $500 each, and Richie got paid off in moth dust. It didn't bother him, though. He was breaking into the big time. Give him a few months and he'd be into diamond rings, two-toned shoes and show girls like the rest of them. Right now it wasn't money he wanted, it was experience.

There was more cloak and dagger to it than that, of course. If Richie didn't show, Louie would phone his house to get the answer. If Louie didn't show, Richie was to go home and wait for a call, and another meeting would be arranged.

Anyway, I had time to kill before standing in for Richie, so I thought I'd wait outside Louie's apartment and see if he was home. I hadn't set eyes on him before, but Richie'd given me a description: fat, balding, black hair, dark glasses, dark suit, a carnation and a cane. He didn't sound easy to miss.

I found a parking slot that gave me a good view and slouched and watched and counted the minutes. There was a clap of thunder and the sky got dark. You don't get many thunderstorms in March, but this was one of the times. Pretty soon there was lightning, then the rain began pelting the pavements and there was a rattle of hailstones on the car roof. Water started running in the gutters and puddles reached out into the street. My windows fogged and I had to crack a port and keep the blower on.

It got to be quarter past five, and traffic grew thick. All the rest of the working stiffs were going home to wife and kiddies. Even Eileen would have locked the office and would be trekking to the bus in her high high heels, with her cute belted raincoat and gaudy umbrella.

I would have missed Louie coming out, what with the traffic and the umbrellas and the hurry, if I hadn't seen the black Cadillac pull in under the portico. Richie had told me about that, as well, even to the license plate. A very cooperative boy, was Richie.

So I leaned forward and rolled down the window for a look. The rain had slackened but it hadn't quit, and I had to share the front seat with it while I watched a uniformed attendant get out and open the passenger door. The Caddy's owner was Louie, all right. Richie's description was more than adequate. But he wasn't alone. He and the attendant were handing a fur-clad female into the front seat, and Louie palmed the attendant a bill before coming around to get behind the wheel. He edged into traffic, and I carved out a place for myself three cars behind. The rain, the traffic and the stoplights didn't matter; following the Caddy was as easy as following a funeral procession. I had to laugh. Louie concealed his pickup points like Russian spies passing microfilm, then made his collections in a car as unobtrusive as a spaceship.

He went into the center of town and out Mendenhall Street to the stiff, gray Shasta Imperial, a brick apartment building that once had made the area the better part of town. That was before urban sprawl and urban decay started the neighborhood downhill. The Shasta Imperial still stood proud, but it was starting to wither. The bricks needed pointing, fluorescent overheads replaced vandalized wall sconces in the lobby, and the plastered wall cracks hadn't been painted.

Louie parked in front to take the lady inside, but I couldn't get close enough to see more than that she had red hair and that her huge fur collar was synthetic.

I left my car double-parked four doors back and ducked through the rain after them. They'd taken the elevator, so I walked in and watched the indicator stop at the fifth floor. There was the sound of doors sliding open and shut, and then after a minute a repeat, and the car started down. Meanwhile I'd looked at the mail slots: there were three apartments up there. Apartments 5A and 5B had male first names; 5C said Rekkart and nothing else. I copied the name into my notebook, turned up the collar of my jacket and loped back to my car.

When Louie climbed into his Caddy again, I was parked on the other side of the street, half a block in front of him.

Louie took a casual drive through back streets, steering clear of the traffic. The rain had stopped and the sky was lightening. Darkness was falling, but not fast enough. I followed the Caddy, varied the distance and all that jazz, but I knew if he had his wits about him, he'd make sure he was rid of me before he'd make a move.

He didn't. He drove down to the docks, and this is a part of town where my heap would be missing its battery, wheels and chrome stripping if I parked it for an hour. Yet there he was in a glistening black luxury sedan that would tempt a saint.

He laid it in and left it in front of a row of empty houses, and when I went by he was pausing on the stoop of number 14 to watch me. I didn't see if he went inside or not, for I had to turn the corner. The time was five of six.

I circled the block, but when I came back his car was gone. I still had fifteen minutes, so I cruised the area. When I picked him up again, he was coming toward me. I didn't look at him when we passed, but he was looking at me.

That was enough of that. I locked up my heap on a side street and went on foot to the shed on the broken-down pier that Richie had told me was where he anted up the envelopes. The description was accurate. The shed had a blue, half-broken door that faced the water. There was a small window with the panes missing on one side; there were a couple of barrels that smelled of dead fish and rotting nets. Richie's job was to wait by the door behind the shed where he'd be out of sight.

That's not where I waited, however. I hid around the corner of the empty warehouse at the head of the pier, twenty feet back of the shed. I took out my gun to check it, holstered it again and waited. That looking-over-my-gun business wasn't to see if it was ready. My gun is always ready. That was only nervousness. The whole place was soaking wet, it was getting dark, and the only light was from some arcs over on the next pier. Everything was silent. It was the kind of spot where you could slit a throat and throw a body over the side, and if the tide were high, the way it was now, with the water lapping at the planks, it wouldn't even make a splash.

And who was this guy who met Richie here every week, Louie the Greek with his black suit, carnation and cane? How dangerous was he? How tough? How stupid or how smart? So you wait, and you aren't really nervous, and you certainly aren't afraid. It's only that you have time to think, and it's the thinking that does it.

I had about twenty minutes of thinking. The first ten minutes I was wondering when he was going to come. The second ten I was wondering *if* he was going to come. When it got to be six twenty-five, I decided this was one of his aborted missions, one of those where Richie was supposed to go home now and wait for a phone call.

And that wasn't going to be so good. Louie

would start checking on things, and his guard would be up.

I moved away from there, but I did it carefully. It wasn't the way I'd come. I went down the dark far side of the warehouse, over the rubbish and broken glass, rusty barrel hoops, dirt, grass and a few rats. I couldn't see them, but I could hear them skitter.

At the front was a broken-down ten-foot fence with a barbed-wire topping. It was bent and decrepit enough that I could squeeze between it and the edge of the warehouse, but I knew it would be hell getting the rust stains off my jacket. No matter; nobody was around, and the only sound was faint singing from a distant saloon.

I picked up my car and circled some more, but there was no sign of the Cadillac. So now what're you going to do, bright boy? He tumbled that you were tailing him and he scrubbed the mission. He smells a double cross. Somebody's after his dough, but he doesn't know who.

I drove slowly back to the Belmore Vista, figuring my future. My plan had been to pick up little Louie, take him to the house I'd rented and pump him dry of information the way I'd pumped Richie. Now Louie had slipped out of my grasp, and he wouldn't be easy to get my hands on again. Meanwhile I couldn't leave Richie unattended forever.

I parked down the block and walked back to the Belmore Vista's glass lobby and indoor fountain. If Louie hadn't come back yet, I could still way-lay him. If he had, maybe I could say I had his collection money and talk him into seeing me. It was a long chance, and he probably wouldn't let me in unless he had some musclemen hiding in the kitchen.

I checked at the desk and found I'd flunked on my first hope. Mr. Bustoni *had* returned to his apartment. There was a house phone in the bank of booths off the elevators, and his pad was 1118. I gave him a ring and was ready with a nice, warm, come-on-type voice that would tell him his money was safe.

Except that when he said, "Hello," his teeth chattered so loudly I forgot to answer.

He said, "Hello," again, and his voice was squeaky. Then he said, "Who's there?"

I hung up quietly. There was no point in going on with it; he was panicking.

I went back to the car and had a cigarette. I don't smoke anymore except once in a great while when I'm up against a real problem. Louie was behind the castle walls with the drawbridge up and the ramparts guarded. Smoke bombs wouldn't drive him out.

I wondered if a woman could.

I flicked the cigarette out the window, brought the heap alive and headed to the Shasta Imperial.

APARTMENT 5C was at the end of the hall, apart from A and B. Since the card in the slot said only Rekkart, when I rang the bell I wondered what would happen if I'd blown another deal and it was a man who answered the door.

I didn't have to have a cigarette over that one, though. A woman's voice said, "What kept you, sweetheart?" and the door was opened. It was the right girl, thick hennaed hair tumbling to her shoulders, the bright lips and coated face. Only this time she wasn't snuggled into a wraparound fur. She was wearing a diaphanous robe and pom-pom mules, with heavily ringed fingers and braceleted wrists. She had a very good-looking body but wasn't prepared to offer it for public inspection, and I concentrated on her mules, rings and false eyelashes.

She didn't scream or even yelp when she found the wrong man on the threshold. All she said was, "What the—" followed by a dirty word. She tried to close the door, of course, and I put a foot in it, of course. She gritted her teeth, and more street-corner words came out between them in a harsher cadence. She didn't scare easily and she wasn't a screamer, but I couldn't waste time on amenities. She'd scream in time, and I wanted to be inside with the door closed when she did.

I threw my weight against the panels and came through. I was rough and went for overkill because I didn't want to have to hit the door twice. I got in all right, and she didn't scream—at least not very loudly. That's because the force of my brutish entry knocked her over the coffee table, dumping her half onto the couch. What came out of her was a yelp of pain. The impact had knocked off a mule and hurt her foot.

Now she held the injured member with one hand and tried to pull the disheveled robe around her with the other. I closed the door behind me, and she watched. She belonged to a special breed. They grow up that way. They're in with the hard guys, like Louie, who're out for the buck. They're out for the buck, too, and they know it's the hard guys you get it from. And they know what they have to do to get it. They're streetwise like nothing you ever saw. And the one thing they've learned in life is, keep your eye on the brass ring.

This kid—she couldn't have been more than twenty-eight, and might only have been an old twenty-two—was on the couch nursing a sore foot, wearing practically nothing at all, alone in an apartment with a stranger who had entered by force. Another girl would have been terrified by the expectancy of rape and robbery. She was not. She'd let you rape her and rob her without a murmur. So what was giving herself to one more slimy male? She'd been doing it since puberty. As for robbery? Nothing she owned she'd paid for herself. The rings and bracelets, even the diaphanous robe, were gifts of someone else. He'd replace them if I took them away.

So now that I had gained admittance, she watched me and massaged her foot and didn't pull the robe as much into place as she could have. Already she was laying out lures. I was a male, and she might divert me from my purpose by making me aware she was a female. I could read her guileless guile even as I approached. It's been the resort of women and the weakness of men since the apple of Eden.

But we men have weapons, too. I didn't look at all she was showing me—at least very much. Instead I concentrated on her eyes. "I got a message for Louie," I said huskily, "and I don't know how to reach him!"

"Louie's in danger?" That brought her upright. Automatically she covered the spots she'd been peekabooing. Now she wanted my thoughts to follow a different course. As for her foot, that didn't hurt anymore.

I nodded knowingly. "The double cross is in, and I know about it. I gotta give him a message."

She was pale as she moved to the phone. "I can reach him. What's the message?"

I came close when she dialed. A silver ID bracelet on her right wrist had the name Sylvia on it. That was what I wanted to see. "What's your name?" she said to me with the phone at her ear.

I shook my head. "No names. Nobody's to know I'm here."

Then she was saying into the mouthpiece, "Honey, are you all right?"

There was an interval of silence while he went into the state of his health. She frowned, and I wondered what he was telling her.

Then it was her turn. "Listen, somebody's here." She cupped the mouthpiece, half turned her back and lowered her voice as if I weren't supposed to hear. "Yes, it's a man. . . . He won't tell me his name. He says it's dangerous." Next she turned back to look me up and down. Louie wanted a description.

I didn't want him matching what she told him with the guy behind the wheel of my heap. I snatched the phone from her and said into it, "Louie, you're in trouble. You know that, don't you?"

His voice was nervous but not squeaky. "Who're you?"

"Didn't Sylvia tell you, no names? Let's just say, do you know a kid named Richie Zullo?"

Louie got careful then. He was groping in the dark and didn't want to break his glasses. "Why? Why're ya asking?"

I said in harsh, tough tones, "Because he's

supposed to have a bundle for you, only he ain't got it." I thought that ought to open his shell a little.

It did. "What happened to it?" he asked cautiously.

"It so happens I got it."

That startled him. It startled the girl, too. She was close enough that I could smell her perfume. She was off to the side, and I turned a little. I didn't want her getting behind me. It wasn't that I didn't trust her; it was a reflex from my cop days.

"You?" he said. "How come?"

"Just doing you a favor," I answered genially. "But I'm not sticking my neck out."

"What's going on? I don't get it."

"I don't, either. Not all of it. And if I did, I wouldn't tell you over the phone."

Sylvia wandered away and began prowling her cage. She was a trifle big in the hips, but she had a swaying, sensual walk. She was gripping her elbows, which pulled the upper half of her robe tight, the better to reveal what was underneath, but I had the feeling she wasn't thinking about that, she was thinking about her future.

Over the phone Louie's sharp, suspicious voice said, "Well, what're you doing? What's your part in this?"

"I'll tell you, Louie," I said. "I thought if I did you a favor, you might do me one."

Now he was on his home ground. I was talking

in his native tongue, and shrewdness came into his voice. "What kind of favor?"

"I've been protecting your interests, Louie. I got some money for you you weren't supposed to get."

"I mean," the icy voice said, "what kind of favor do you want from me?" He was in charge now, and the whole character of his voice had changed. You'd never have guessed he could squeak.

"I'm hoping you might like to hire me to keep on protecting your interests. Of course," I added, "if you don't fancy the idea, then maybe you might give me a little reward for the dough I saved for you, and keep me in mind."

He was pegging me now, sifting me through his strainer, figuring where I fitted into the scheme of things. He was starting to like my pigeonhole. I was smart enough but dumb enough. I'd thwarted some kind of "fix Louie" scheme he wasn't onto, which showed I was smart, but at the same time I didn't realize my worth, which was dumb. That gave him the best of both worlds, and he could play with that. A touch of warmth came into his voice. "You don't have to worry," he assured me. "Louie Bustoni always pays his debts!"

It sounded like the start of a beautiful friendship. I said, "That's why I went to bat for you, Louie. I figured you were the kind of guy who was good to his friends."

"Ya got me pegged right, pal," he told me. "Say, what's your name again?"

Slick Louie.

"I ain't tellin' ya my name," I said, with hostile suspicion in my own voice, "until we make a deal. And I mean, signed in blood!"

He laughed. He even laughed! I should take up acting!

"That's right," he said. "Mr. X. Signed in blood."

"You got it." I waited for him to take it from there.

He came on again. "You say you got my dough?"

"Some. Maybe not all. It depends on how much you're missing."

"And if some is missing?"

"I'll get it for ya."

He liked me better by the minute. "Yeah, well, I can see you're a guy I want to meet. Where're ya been all these years?"

"Waiting for a chance to show what I can do."

Sylvia was sizing me up during this little chat, trying to get her priorities straight. Girls like Sylvia survive by knowing which way to jump and when. I could tell by the clicking wheels behind her eyes that she was measuring distance and time. For the first time she was picturing Louie on the back burner.

Into the phone Louie was saying, "You're at Sylvia's—say, how the hell do you know Sylvia?"

"Nothing over the phone, Louie," I said. "I told you that."

He grumbled as his mind cast among her acquaintances for a clue. "Listen, fella, I want to see ya."

"That's right," I said. "As soon as you can get here—"

"Hey, now, wait—"

"This money's getting hot and I can't hold it much longer."

"Yeah, well—okay. Let me talk to Sylvia."

"I'll give you twenty minutes. Otherwise I'll be gone."

"Well, now, hey, wait—"

I held out the phone and Sylvia came close for it, so close her protuberances rubbed against me. "Yeah, honey?"

She turned away when she talked so I couldn't see her expression, and her voice was flat. She said yes, I was here, and was he coming over, and it went on like that. Then she replaced the phone and looked up at me. "He'll be right over," she told me. "Twenty minutes, like you said."

"Great."

She lingered there, waiting. For what? For me to make a move? Was she trying to stock the larder a little fuller? What did she think we were going to do in twenty minutes, with time enough after to make it appear we hadn't done anything?

I took her by the arm. "And I think what you'd better do, dear girl," I said, "is go get into your best party dress. I don't think Louie'd like you entertaining strangers in that outfit."

The thought made her shudder. "Yeah," she said. "Louie's got no imagination." She went for the bedroom.

And I very quietly went for the elevator.

8

WHEN LOUIE LOCKED UP THE CADILLAC in front of the Shasta Imperial, I came out of the bushes by the side. He turned around, and even in the dim of the streetlights he was wearing his silvered glasses. You've really got to be scared of what your eyes will say when you even hide them at night.

Louie couldn't've been long in the rackets. He didn't have bodyguards; he didn't drag the field before he landed; he didn't do anything to protect himself. All he did was flaunt a Caddy, a broad, a pad in the Belmore Vista, tailored clothes, cane, carnation and silvered glasses. He blew his earnings on plumes rather than armor.

Poor Louie.

I stuck a gun in his ribs when he turned around. There was nobody on the streets, and the night man at the Shasta Imperial was reading a newspaper in the lobby.

Louie's mouth hung loose, and I plucked off his glasses to get a look at his eyes. That gave him a look at me, and I saw recognition flicker. I was the one behind the wheel of the heap.

His legs almost gave way as he realized he'd been double-crossed by the double-crosser. "Back'n the car, Louie," I said, sliding a hand over his clothes. "Hold it just a minute." I relieved him of a small pistol in the pocket of his overcoat, and a larger one in a holster over his heart. I'd get to the lesser items later.

I made him open the doors, put him in front and me in back and told him where to drive. I sat on the jump seat breathing down his neck, and we went out to my little house in the country.

The place was dark, the yard was empty, the night was still. I made Louie kill the lights and motor and I took the keys. Then I shone my small pocket flash and moved into the front seat with him. From the way the sweat was pouring down his face, he was wondering if all the perks—the suite, the broad, the car and the rest—were worth it. I wondered if he would wet his pants like Richie.

"All right," I said. "Now we're gonna talk."

What I wanted from him, I said, were the names of all the other Richie Zullos who did his dirty work for him. I wanted to know the names of all his customers, how much he squeezed them for each week, what his cut was, whom he turned the dough over to, and who was Mr. Big in the racket. It was asking a lot. It was asking more than he knew and much more than he wanted to tell, but he was even more cooperative than Richie. I didn't have to fire my gun, I only had to club him with it a little, start the blood flowing down his cheek and out of his nose. I think I might have loosened a tooth or two, but I doubt it. He didn't require the full treatment. Like Richie, he started to cry.

Along with the tears he spilled his guts, and I wrote it all down. Eileen would have been impressed with my speed. I got all the names of his helpers. There were four of them, and each was shaking down four establishments, and it was neat what the protection price was. There must have been a researcher in the gang, for the figures Louie gave me were, as best I could judge, close to the maximum the gang could skim off without driving the owner out of business. They left him just enough profit to tempt him not only to pay, but to keep quiet.

Only in the case of the Rafes was the ante out of line. It was at the choke-off level, and Louie's bosses were going to lose a customer if they didn't reevaluate the squeeze.

The main thing I was after, though, was the name of Louie's superior. Whom did he turn over his dough to—was it the big boss, or was it some intermediary?

All Louie could give me was a name: Benny Wyckoff, a short, stout man who lived in the Parkview Plaza, a swanker apartment even than Louie's. Louie didn't know anything about him except that he paid a visit there every Friday morning and handed over such and such an amount of money—the total from his collections—and it came to just over three thousand a week. Figure Louie was collecting from sixteen contributors per week and you get the idea.

I took him inside the house with a gun in his back and my pocket flash for a guide. The beam picked out Richie Zullo. He was where I'd left him, wrists fastened to either end of the radiator, ankles bound, restraining lines also fastened to the radiator. I'd left him with enough slack so that he could shift position a little, but not enough for him to do anything worthwhile.

Richie's face was white in the sharp glow of the flash, his cheeks stained. He'd been crying some more. The moment the light hit him, he shrieked, "Oh, God, help me! Please help me!" He was afraid of the dark, especially all tied up.

Then Louie said, "You!" like an oath, and that stopped him.

Richie stared into the flash as we advanced, and then he could see who it was. "Louie!" The fear he had of the dark was nothing like the fear he now felt. "Louie, Louie," he sobbed, "I didn't tell him. I swear I didn't."

Louie launched a kick that would've broken Richie in two except that I clubbed him and he tripped instead and cut his head open on the sideboard.

"Oh, God, oh, God," Richie kept saying while I clapped handcuffs on his former pal and wrestled him onto the bed. Louie was stunned and half-out, but when his strength returned he started struggling against the cuffs and turning so red in the face I thought he was going to burst an artery and I'd have a corpse on my hands. He was wrestling and kicking at me, trying to get to Richie. He was going to kill Richie for ratting, without realizing he'd just done the same thing himself.

There was nothing for it but to conk him with a gun butt, and since I was out of practice, I had to do it twice. You have to be careful rapping people on the skull. You get enthusiastic and you're going to spill brains and everything gets very messy. So you tend to crack them tentatively that first time, testing their skull against the weapon, evaluating the effect, so that the second time you can produce the desired result.

My desired result was to lay Louie out like the guest of honor at a wake, quiet and peaceful, with no anger showing. That done, I put away the handcuffs and got out the clothesline, tying his hands and feet to the four posts of the bed. Then I went through a thorough search for the rest of the armaments he carried, which netted me a pair of brass knuckles, a switchblade and a belt buckle that had a wedge-shaped knife attached.

Richie was watching me through all this as if I were a surgeon doing a heart transplant. I tended to him once I had Louie restrained. I showed him my gun—one of my guns—untied him and gave him fifteen minutes to have a bite to eat, something to drink, and to use the facilities. Then I tied him back up. Through it all he tried to get me to take him away from there—away from Louie, away from the dark and imagined rats. I just let him talk.

By this time Louie was awake. Louie wasn't so angry with Richie anymore as he was afraid of me. He was beginning to understand the spot Richie'd been in and was starting to worry about his own skin.

"What're ya gonna do?" he asked, and his voice was getting squeaky once more.

There was no point in answering, and I said, "I'll be back in the morning. Don't bother yelling. Nobody can hear you."

I turned for the door, and Louie said croakily, "How much d'ya want?"

"Good night," I said. "Sweet dreams."

I opened the door, and he called out, "I ain't kidding. I'm talking real dough."

I paused. "How real?"

"How about a hundred grand?"

I laughed.

"I swear. One hundred grand to turn us loose."

"You aren't carrying even one grand."

"Not on me, but I can get it for you."

I didn't believe him and I didn't want to waste any more time. "Tell me about it in the morning," I said, and went out locking the door behind me.

9

I STOPPED BY THE OFFICE to chuck my gun and change wallets. The new wallet identified me as Henry Marvin and carried calling cards describing me as a sales representative, without specifying the products line. From there I drove Louie's Caddy to the quarters of Father Jack McGuire.

It was half-past ten now and there weren't any lights on, but I rang the bell anyway because priests are supposed to be like God—on duty twenty-four hours a day.

It took a while, but then the outside light came on and Mrs. Honeywell opened the door. She's Father Jack's housekeeper, and she and her husband have a suite below stairs. She said, "Oh, it's you, Mr. Kaye. I couldn't imagine who'd be bothering Father McGuire at this hour." She said protectively, "He's retired, Mr. Kaye. He's had a hard day. Is it important?"

I said it was extremely important and came in. She sighed and said, very well, she would ring. I said I could do it myself. Then a light appeared down the hall, and Jack was there in lounging robe and pajamas. "I should've known it'd be you," he said. "It's all right, Mrs. Honeywell."

She had to accept that and went back to her quarters. I went down, and Jack took me into his study, which is where we usually play chess. In fact, the chessboard was in position under its low-hanging overhead. "I don't suppose," he said, glancing at the board, "that you've come for a game."

"Your nonsuppositions are in good form tonight."

"You're not about to give yourself to Jesus Christ, I can detect that. The only other reason you're here must be that you're in trouble."

"You sound like Mycroft Holmes."

"Does it have anything to do with that Cadillac you arrived in?"

"You were peeking."

"When the doorbell rang I did look out the window. When I saw the car I didn't expect you. The two don't fit."

"There's a long story to be told, and I don't have much time."

"And this is not a confession, right? You want me to do something for you, right?"

"You don't let me have any fun. You know all the answers before I even ask the questions."

Jack sat down behind his desk and cupped his fingers over his nose. "I can tell I'm not going to like it," he said. "You never bring me anything I like."

"Of course not," I said. "People don't go to doctors except when they're sick. And they don't go to priests except when they're in trouble. What do you think? It's too late to play chess!"

"You're wrought up," he said reflectively. He raised himself in the chair and his manner became brisker. "What is it?"

I gave him the story very fast: about the Rafes, about Doria, about Richie Zullo and Louie the Greek, about Sylvia Rekkart and Benny Wyckoff. "I think Benny's only another steppingstone," I said. "I don't think he's Mr. Big."

Jack shook his head. "No, he isn't."

My ears perked up. "You know something?"

He shook his head again. "I hear bits and pieces, not enough to get a picture, but enough to get some of the parts. Benny Wyckoff's up in the rackets. I've heard the name. But he's not it." Jack looked at me. "I'll tell you one thing, though. He's someone to stay away from."

"He's that high up, huh?"

"If that's the way you want to put it."

"Okay, that's why I wanted to see you. Those punks I've got locked up in the house I rented—"

"That's kidnapping. You know that, don't you?"

"I'm confessing. You're held to silence."

"I also can't aid and abet. But I can tell you to forget it."

I stood up. "I didn't come here for advice, God damn it. I've put two punks temporarily out of commission just so I can move up the ladder to the next punk—"

"And when you get to him?"

"I put him out of commission and go on to the next. And so on until I get to the top dog."

"And then what?"

"I'll worry about that when I come to it. I'll tell you one thing, though. I'm going to put him out of commission."

"Or he'll put you out of commission."

"He'll try."

"He's more likely to win than you are. He's got money, and he's got people who'll do what he wants. What've you got?"

"You."

Jack had been serious before. Now he was going to get really serious.

I cut him off. "It's all very simple," I said. "I'm going to see Benny Wyckoff. I'm telling you this not to involve you, but so you'll know what to tell the police if I don't come back. And also so you can get some help to those punks I've got tied up in that house. I can't let them starve to death. They deserve it, but that's only my personal opinion. Your superchief up in the sky might have a different view, and I'll let Him have the say. But you're not to move on any of this unless you haven't heard from me by ten o'clock tomorrow morning. At that time call out the marines. Okay?"

Jack shook his head. "You're determined, aren't you? Don't bother answering. And you won't listen to reason, either, will you? And don't answer that, either. Answer this question instead. How much are you being paid for this enterprise?"

I said, "I don't know. I'm getting something. Maybe it's a week's payment out of the Rafes. If they can afford it. I forget."

"You're dumping assignments in my lap in case you're not alive tomorrow morning. And for what?"

"What're you talking about? You have to take chances in this world. Otherwise life's not worth living."

"You know what you are, you dumb stupid jerk? You're Sir Galahad in quest of the Holy Grail."

I said, "Trust you to bring religion into it. Next thing you'll be doing is asking me to pray before I go see Benny."

"All right, forget religion. You're Don Quixote and you're going out to tilt against windmills. Because that's what you're doing, you dumb cluck. You think you're going to wipe out evil, all by your little old self. And it's not going to happen. Evil will exist on this planet long after you and I have gone."

"Say, does the Pope know about you?"

Jack said sadly, "I'm not saying you shouldn't fight against evil. You should. But you should plan your efforts to produce the maximum effect over the longest period of time."

"Very good," I said. "Except that I'm not doing this because I'm Sir Galahad or Don Quixote. I'm doing it because Doria Rafe has great big beautiful troubled eyes, and I want to take the trouble away."

10

BENNY LIVED at the address Louie had given me. Not that I doubted it. Louie was the kind of guy who'd lie, but not when he could be punished for it.

I left Louie's Cadillac on a side street and walked half a block. The apartment was another of those extravaganzas where the lobby is a glassed-in football field with a ceiling Mickey Mantle couldn't hit with a bat and ball.

There was a check-in desk where guests, delivery boys, salesmen, hookers—anybody who wasn't a resident—had to state their business and get it confirmed by a phone call and a pass. It was a touch of little old New York.

A couple in tuxedo and gown were ahead of me, and when I said, "Benny Wyckoff's apartment, please," the clerk looked over my clothes with distaste, then said, "Eighteen D. Follow the other couple."

That was interesting. Nobody told me to check my gun, or even asked if I had one. Nobody wanted my name or phoned on ahead to alert the sentries. It appeared I'd chosen a night when

Benny was entertaining and the restrictions were being short-circuited.

I got into the elevator with the other couple, who avoided me by going in for some mumbo jumbo about had they remembered to turn off the gold taps in the bathtub. They were groomed and tweezered, powdered and perfumed, like French poodles the night before the dog show, and didn't like sharing their cage with a mongrel.

On the eighteenth floor I followed them down the hall, they behaving as if I were some mendicant they couldn't shake. Then they were stepping inside a door and being clapped on the shoulder—at least, the man was being clapped on the shoulder—by a burly simian in his first tuxedo. They were admitted like old friends, but the burly type turned back into place like a swinging door when I attempted to follow.

"Where's your ticket?" he said with a scowl that came down almost to the tip of his nose. He had three inches and fifty pounds on me, plus the advantage of the tuxedo, and he sensed that at last he didn't have to defer.

"Oh, yes," I said, and explored some pockets. "I must have left it in my other suit." (I was going to say "tuxedo," but caught myself.)

"Too bad," he said, as if that ended the conversation.

I took out one of my Henry Marvin cards and scribbled on the back, "I'll be subbing for Louie the Greek," then handed it to him. "Show this to Benny," I said. "He's going to want to see me."

Monster Man studied the card, trying to get the message. "What's it mean?"

"Ask Benny."

"This ain't no admittance card. You can't get in with this." He pushed the card back at me.

"Benny gives me orders," I told him. "Not you. And if you don't believe it, wait and see what happens if you don't give him that card."

That unnerved him enough to pass the card to a backup semigorilla with the curt order to give it to Benny. Then he resumed his Colossus of Rhodes stance and pretended I wasn't there.

Three or four more bedecked couples arrived while I waited, and the party looked like a good mix: low-lifes and high-lifes, modern-day thieves mingling with those whose grandparents were the thieves. There was a burble of sound inside and the muted strains of a decent combo.

Finally the smaller of the guardians came back, still holding my card. He whispered to Big Boy and used the card to beckon me forward.

We went across the vestibule to a door beside the entrance hall. The room at the far end of the hall was jammed with black ties and evening gowns, white-jacketed waiters and tinkling glasses. There was noise, music and the chatter of a good time. That was for the guests, not for the likes of me. I was taken through the near door into a small paneled study complete with desk, couch, a couple of chairs and plate-glass windows that looked out over the whole of the city.

Two youngish but tough-looking men in tuxedos were waiting for me there, and my leader deposited me in their care without a word. The door closed behind me and that was it.

The two youths weren't like Gargantua and Son of Gargantua out in the vestibule. They might not feel truly comfortable in tuxedos, but they were comfortable in their surroundings and in their business. They weren't pushover types like Richie Zullo and Louie the Greek. They were pros, and they didn't have to tell you. It showed in how they handled themselves and what they did. They didn't pull guns on me; they didn't have to. They didn't even have to act tough.

"All right, hands on your head," the near one said. He was a blond Nordic type with a scar down one cheek. He stood in front of me, and the other moved behind so I couldn't keep them both in view. I can tell you, that's a good way to get me to put my hands on my head.

When I did that, the Swede opened my coat and went through pockets while the one behind slid his hands all over my back, chest, hips and legs. It was quick, it was efficient. They came away with my gun (Louie's gun, actually), my billfold (the one calling me Henry Marvin), the keys to the Caddy, and my pocketknife. If I'd had additional weapons strapped to my legs and arms, they would have had them, too.

The gun and the stuff from my pockets they put on the desk. Then they made me sit in the leather chair opposite and took positions behind me, one on each side. They didn't gloat about the haul; they didn't chide me for walking into Benny's with a gun in my pocket.

Now the opposite door opened, letting in sounds of the party, and Benny Wyckoff entered quickly, closing it behind. He looked harried, impatient and irritable. He went over the items on top of the desk, making a face at the gun—it wasn't a weapon somebody who knew about guns would choose—picking up my wallet and going through it with hasty disregard. He knew by looking at me that the gun wasn't mine, and he knew nothing in the wallet would be mine, either. To tell the truth, I wasn't even myself at that moment.

I'd been playing tag with the likes of Richie Zullo and Louie the Greek, and they make you sloppy. I'd underestimated the next rung of the ladder. Benny and his crew weren't fooled by anything I'd shown them so far, and I was going to have to do a helluva lot of fast talking to get out of there under my own power.

Benny, after he'd dispensed with my credentials, sat down behind the desk and gave me his undivided attention; and I can tell you it's not the kind of look you want to get from Benny—not unless you're the one who's on top.

"All right," he said, "be fast. What's this all about?"

He had thinning dark hair and slit eyes, a square jaw and heavy jowls, except that the heaviness was muscle, not fat. He looked as if he could chew nails—the galvanized kind, not hangnails.

I didn't think the humble approach would work. To tell the truth, I didn't think any kind of approach would work and I wondered where I'd be by the time Jack McGuire called for the bloodhounds.

I didn't let myself dwell on that; self-pity doesn't buy you any tears but your own. A nice, forthright, innocent air was called for by the occasion. I tried my best to be forthright and innocent.

"I understand you and Louie the Greek aren't going to be doing business together anymore and—"

Benny Wyckoff was one man who didn't need silvered glasses to keep his eyes from betraying him. I was giving him an opening gambit that would have rocked a stone Buddha, and not a muscle twitched. I really had to hand it to him, and I wondered what my chances were if I found it desirable to take a dive through one of his eighteenth-floor plate-glass windows. There are worse things than dying, and I had the feeling Benny Wyckoff knew what they were.

So I was left hanging on my "and," expecting him to be interrupting with all kinds of questions. But he just looked at me as at a bug and I was left to finish on my own. "And—well, I'd like to be considered as a possible replacement."

I stopped. He or somebody else was going to have to take it from there. I'd contributed my share. In fact, I thought of standing up and saying, "Thank you very much, keep me in mind," and trying to get out, except I knew I wasn't going anywhere.

Benny finally spoke. "Who's Louie the Greek?" he asked, sounding as if he'd really like to know.

I tried about the only option I had. "The guy who comes to pay you off every Friday morning."

That fetched me a whack on the side of the head from the non-Swedish bodyguard who was dark and mean-looking. For a second I didn't know where I was. Then I tried to jump to my feet. There's one thing I want people to know. Nobody pushes me around. Except for present company. These two intended to push me around plenty, and that was only the opening scene of act one. I wasn't halfway up before both of the bodyguards had me rammed back down so deep in the seat my fanny must've made an imprint on the springs.

Benny, in a smooth-as-silk voice, said, "Say that again."

"Louie the Greek pays you off every Friday."

I got clubbed again so hard my head rang.

"Try it again," Benny said, like a teacher who really wanted the student to improve.

I swallowed and tried to remember what it was he'd asked me. "Benny—I mean, Louie—he comes to—visit you on Fridays. I think."

I was braced, but this time I didn't get clobbered.

"How do you know this?" Benny said in his silky voice.

"Louie told me."

"Where's Louie?"

"I don't know."

For a while there things were going fine. But that was an answer he didn't like. His eyebrow lifted and I caught another fist on the temple.

I must've blacked out for a couple of seconds, then all I knew about was a throbbing sensation in my head and a blurred Benny facing me across the desk.

He said something, but I didn't quite hear it. Then behind him the door opened and the noise of the party came through. Also coming through was a bosomy, full-fleshed brass blonde in a white strapless gown with an orchid corsage. She was more of a vision than a picture, for my eyesight was foggy, and her words sounded as if they were being sifted through oatmeal.

"Benny," she said irritably, going to him without seeing anyone else, "you've got to come back out. I can't handle those gorilla friends of yours all by myself." She pointed here and there to apparently damaged spots and said, "Do you want my dress to be ruined?"

BENNY WAVED HER AWAY. "I'm busy." He aimed a finger at me. "All right," he said in a voice turned viperish, "what's your angle?"

The blonde with the brass hair tossed her head and flumped herself down on the couch. "Well, I'm not going back out there by myself," she said sulkily. "I can tell you that."

"Shut up," Benny said. "I'm talking." He aimed his finger again. "Let's hear it, funny man."

"No angle," I replied, hoping a soft answer would turneth away wrath. "Louie asked me to fill in for him, that's all."

Benny made beckoning motions with his fingers. "C'mon, c'mon. Let's hear the whole of it."

"I don't know much more than that. He had to leave town, sudden like, and he needed someone to take his place for a few days."

Benny didn't like it. I was going to get slugged again. It makes you tense up and get a little nervous. I talked some more, very quickly. "He needed somebody to take up the collections for him. He said the delivery date is Friday. Friday morning." I was watching Benny's eyes, and they weren't giving me any come-ons. Could that creep Louie have lied to me after all? Did I have the date wrong?

"He gave me a list of the, ah, customers, too," I said, and my voice sounded funny.

Benny pushed the contents of my pockets around on his desk. "Any money on him?" he asked his handy-dandy assistants.

One of them, I think it was the Swede, said, "Only what's in his wallet."

That wasn't much, of course. I wasn't risking more dough than necessary on this enterprise. Benny regarded me with what, if it were someone else, would be called a thoughtful look. "So Louie picked you, that's what you want us to believe, is that it?"

I nodded. The girl on the couch had produced a compact from her sash and was lathering on the lipstick. I didn't know girls used the stuff anymore, but she did—lots of it. She had crossed her knees and she could have been alone in the room for all the attention she paid to the conversation.

"Louie's going to tell *you* he's leaving town, but he's not telling me, is that it? He picks his own stand-in without clearing it with anybody. Is that it?"

I shrugged. "Well, you know Louie. If I were in your shoes, I'd pick a brainier guy." I gave him a bright smile. "Like me."

It didn't go over. "You think he's dumb, you're dumber! Coming up here with that crappy story.

You think I'm gonna believe a crappy story like that?''

''Listen,'' I said, ''what the hell would I be coming up here for otherwise? You think I come up here because I like getting beat up?''

That gave him something to think about. Daniel doesn't walk into the lion's den to make a meal out of himself. I had to have an angle. He didn't like the one I'd given him, but he didn't have a better one.

He regarded me for about ten taut seconds—taut for everybody in the room except for the blonde. Now she was smearing on the rouge and powder.

Finally he picked up his phone and dialed a number. He swung his chair enough to look out at the city lights. The bodyguards stood at the ready behind me, I sat at the ready trying not to think about the future, and the girl evaluated her makeup technique with the aid of the compact mirror.

There was no answer. He tired of it, swung back, depressed the phone button and dialed another number. This time he hitched the chair closer to the desk, took a distasteful look at my gun, then pushed it aside and flipped open the wallet. Into the phone he said, ''This is Benny. Is the chief there?''

There was another wait while Benny fingered the wallet. Then he spoke again, and now his tone was deferential. ''Chief, sorry to bother you, but something's come up and I've got a question. The name Henry Marvin mean anything to you?'' He looked me over and said, ''About six feet, a hundred and ninety, dark hair. Young—youngish. He's not a kid. Carries an automatic. Calls himself a salesman.''

A pause followed. Then Benny's eyes met mine. ''Don't know nothing about him, huh?'' The eyes were like broken glass. ''Well, he knows something about us!''

He listened one more time, then he said, ''Don't worry, I'll find out,'' and hung up. ''All right,'' he said, rising, ''now we're gonna get some answers.'' He gestured to his army. ''Stand him up.''

I was yanked to my feet, my arms pinioned at my sides. Benny came around the desk, brushing against the big blonde's knees. She looked up and put her compact away. Now she was back from never-never land. It was as if on cue.

''Okay,'' Benny said, advancing on me, ''you're gonna talk straight.'' He came without stopping, arching back a fist to let me have it right in the kisser with all his might. He could have had his men do it for him, but he wanted to get into the act. He had some hate to unleash, and who knows, maybe he thought it would impress the blonde.

She squealed, ''Benn-eee,'' when he wound up. Except then she squealed, ''Donnnn't!''

He didn't. I let him have it first.

The gestapo agents had my arms, but I could brace my feet. I caught him with the point of my shoe where I meant to catch him, and he never threw that punch. He went down instead, and the scream he let out, if the windows had been open, could have been heard in Canada, but with the doors closed and the noise of the party to boot, he wasn't even heard in the next room.

He squiggled around on the floor, clutching himself and kicking like a beetle on its back. Blondie, appalled, went to her knees to hug him to her, but he wouldn't hold still. "Oh, Benneee," she moaned in anguish. Maybe she was worried about his future need for her.

The black-tied gestapo agents had other thoughts. Their captive had just creamed their boss and they had their own future to worry about. Each of them slammed a fist into my belly as if they were trying to find my spine. I went back against the wall so hard I thought I was going through. Fortunately, my skull is thick—they don't call me "bonehead" for nothing—and the crack of skull against plaster didn't hurt me as much as it sounded.

I went down, though. But only for a moment. They yanked me to my feet so hard I almost fell on top of Benny. I was groggy for a moment—like when you're in the ring and catch one you didn't see coming; there's that split-second shudder, and then you have your wits about you again. It was like that, except I didn't think my wits were going to do me much good. I'd had the pleasure of crippling the boss, but I knew he'd take it out on me ten times over. And his henchmen had to make sure that happened.

The swarthy one was holding me upright, and the Swede was slipping his fingers into a pair of brass knuckles. What was going to happen next promised to be awful messy. I'd get inured to the pain, but there'd be a lot of blood and broken bones, and if I lived through it I wouldn't have a lot of teeth.

Then the blonde, not getting anywhere with Benny, saw what the Swede was going to do, and she shrieked again. She scrambled to her feet just as he reared back to let me have it, and latched onto his arm with both of hers. "No! You'll kill him!" she was screaming.

The force of his effort pulled her around with him into the swarthy hood who was holding me. She went to the floor, he staggered, I got free, and the Swede lurched back and tripped over Benny's feet.

The whole place was a shambles, like something in a comedy movie, except that the mood in that room crackled with rage, anxiety and hate.

I got the first blow in. The moment I wrestled an arm free from the black-haired hood, all my functions seemed to fuse. I wasn't groggy anymore, my ribs didn't ache anymore, I didn't feel like throwing up anymore. I'd been given a chance and I didn't have to be told it was the last one I'd get. I hit Blackie a karate chop that was higher than I meant. It was supposed to get his throat but caught his jaw, and it was hard. I could feel the bone give, and he went flat on his back.

I wanted his gun, but there wasn't time. I was afraid the Swede would have his unsheathed. He didn't. It was the blonde he was after, and the expression on his face made her scream and scramble.

He was on his knees and swung the brass knuckles. It was only a glancing blow above the ear, but it knocked her against the couch and left her shrieking in terror. Then he pounced, and as he came out of his crouch, I gave him a soccer kick with everything I had.

My foot caught him in the chest, bringing him full to his feet but throwing him off balance, and he staggered back. The heating system in the building runs along the outside walls. It's a vaned hot-water pipe in a box eighteen inches high and a foot inside the glass panes. He tripped over it going backward, so when he hit the plate glass he went right through. There was an explosion of bursting pane, and great chunks of window disappeared into the blackness with him. Cold night air came through the hole, bearing his frantic fading scream as he dropped. It was eighteen floors and we never heard the thud.

There wasn't time to wait for it, either. Blondie was stunned and staring on the couch, blood streaming down the left side of her face, her mouth agape, her stark gaze fixed on the gaping hole in the window, her face drained bloodless under the pink and orange of her makeup. She didn't know what she'd started and couldn't believe what was happening.

Benny, though, didn't sit and stare. That's not how to climb the ladder of success, and he, crippled and in pain, was fighting back. He had dragged himself to his feet and was going for my gun on the desk.

I jumped on him, threw him onto the couch and grabbed it myself—that and the rest of my things. He lay groaning on the cushions, struggling to recoup while I pocketed everything in sight. Blackie, on the floor, was out of it. Blondie, bleeding and crying beside the agonized Benny, was dazed and a mess. Even so, she reached out a comforting hand to him and said, "Honey, are you all right?"

That was all it took. He went berserk. He let out a yell. He belted her in the mouth, then caught her in the eye and side of the jaw with two more punches before I got to him. She was whimpering and he was cursing.

I yanked him off her and threw him against the wall. I can curse, too, and let him have a broadside, and I pistol-whipped him while I did. He screamed, cried, struggled, and the blood flowed. I'm really the kind, noble type, but I forget myself in the clinches.

I also forgot about Miss Tenderheart. She jumped on me, shrieking, "Don't kill him, don't kill him," and grabbed my arm. It was the same way she'd grabbed the Swede's arm and it had the same effect. Benny got free.

He didn't come for me, though. He went the other way, tearing open the door to the party room and rushing screaming out to where all the music and drinking and laughter and talk were going on.

I can tell you that stopped everybody dead. A sea of faces turned and gaped at the frightened stumbling figure with the blood streaming down his face, then stared in at where big bully Simon Kaye was standing, gun in hand, blood in eye.

Right then nobody moved, but I knew in a moment the reserves would be mustered. I grabbed the blonde by the wrist, said, "Come on, run like hell," and dragged her after me, over Blackie's motionless form, and through the vestibule door.

A well-dressed couple who looked fresh from the opera was being saluted by the tuxedoed bouncer. I showed my gun as an exit visa and it got us into the hall. We jumped aboard the elevator just before the doors closed.

I barely had time to put my gun away before I had to catch the blond girl in my arms. She'd fainted dead away.

12

I HAD HER AWAKE ENOUGH TO FUNCTION by the time we hit the lobby, and walked her through as if she were my drunken sister. I could have carried her on my head for all the attention we would have attracted. The Swede and half the eighteenth-floor window had landed in the alley, and all hell was breaking loose.

Outside in the air the blonde recovered enough to walk to the Caddy with only my hand under her arm. She was still in shock, though. An ambulance and a couple of police cruisers came screaming up the street, and she shook her head. "Everybody hurting everybody. Everybody bleeding and crying. And Jan, he's dead. Oh, God, it can't be real. I can't stand people getting hurt. I'm going out of my mind."

She slumped into the passenger seat when I opened the door and she started to cry, her face in her hands. I got in, slipped the key into the ignition, then sat with her and waited till the shock wore off. After about five minutes she lifted her head, the tears still flowing, and looked at her stained fingers. "My God," she said, "I'm bleeding."

"You got hurt, too," I reminded her.

She laid her head against the seat. "I didn't know it would be like this." She choked on a sob. "I didn't know it would be like this."

I started the engine, shifted into drive and let the wheels take us away. Her breathing steadied, and after a couple of minutes the motion of the car got through to her and she said, without a great deal of curiosity and with no alarm, "Where're we going? Where're you taking me?"

"Where d'you live?"

Her eyes popped wide open and she sat up straight. She was back in the real world again. "We aren't going there," she said in fright. "We aren't going there. Benny would kill me."

"He's not exactly going to love you the way things stand now," I said.

"Oh, God, I wish I was dead. Why did I get mixed up in Benny's business? Why didn't I go back to the party like I should have?"

"Frankly," I said, "I'm glad you didn't. Otherwise I'd probably be the one who went out the window."

She shuddered and covered her face. "Oh, Christ. Why did it have to happen? Jan was an all right guy. Now he's dead."

"He was a prince."

She turned. "You didn't know him. You didn't know what he was like."

"I was finding out the hard way."

She buried her face again. "Oh, Christ, what am I going to do?" She looked at me. "Maybe if I went back and apologized. Maybe I—"

I laughed. "Benny's going to be up to his armpits in cops. You'd be as welcome as the black plague."

"But I can't just ride around—"

"That's right."

"But you can't take me home. You can't know where I live. Then I could never make it right with Benny." She had a bright idea. "Let me off right here. I can find a cab."

She was a dreamer. I gave her the high hard glower. "Come down out of the clouds. You and I are gonna talk, doll face. I didn't save your hide just because I like girls. If you're afraid to have me taint your villa, that's okay. We can go somewhere else. You got a place in mind, or do you want me to pick one?"

She left it to me, and I found a small cocktail lounge in an unfamiliar part of town. I sent her to the ladies' so she could repair the damage to her scalp, and had her whiskey-sour order waiting when she came back, the blood all gone and a fresh coat of face paint in place. I toasted her with my Scotch for saving my life, and she hardly heard me. She went through the whiskey sour as if the glass had a hole in the bottom. A second one was slower and took two gulps.

Her neck and shoulders were getting some color back. Her face, of course, had already been taken care of. She was feeling better; which didn't mean she was better off, it only meant she was getting over the shakes.

As she came down out of the trees, she grew

more cooperative. Her name, she said, was Lizabeth Lynch, and she'd been Benny's girl for just under six months.

I fed her a third whiskey sour, and she found me more likable by the minute. I reminded her of an uncle who died when she was seven. The way the drinks were hitting her, it invested me with family membership and she started to tell me her life story. I was only interested in the past six months of it, but she was into the big scene—the pets that had died, the shingle tombstone for the dead robin, the first day in school, the first boy who kissed her, the first to lay her, the Juliet role in the school play that had been fraudulently denied her—her boobs were unquestionably bigger than the winner's—the development of her career—bed to bed—culminating in her success at landing, as her most recent and finest benefactor, none other than Benny Wyckoff.

His was the ultimate scalp—at least, as of this moment. In a year or two, if she could have stayed the distance, she'd probably have been reaiming her sights. Right now, though, Benny was the crowning glory of a limited ambition. She was so pleased with her achievement, and so worried about what she'd done to her future by grabbing Jan's arm, that you wanted to cry. She was berating herself for a noble instinct, but she lived in a milieu in which noble instincts would undo you. The pity was, she didn't yet realize it.

What Benny's punishment would be occupied her mind. Perhaps if she kept her clothes off she could distract him. Perhaps if she lost those extra pounds she'd been meaning to lose since he got her living it up. . .? Maybe she could learn new sexual techniques, or how to wave her charms at him more alluringly. The body beautiful was her only weapon and her only defense. She didn't think in terms of anything else. In fact, the more she leaned on me, the more she gave me peeks down the front of her gown. Yet she wouldn't have let me in her bedroom if I broke all her teeth. In Benny's world—which was where she lived—that would be the kiss of death. She was trying to do with her body what so many girls do: eat her cake and have it, too. Lure, but stay pure!

All of this was fascinating if you're a sociologist. Well, hell, private detectives don't mind it, either. But what I wanted out of Lizabeth Lynch wasn't the story of a dead robin or a dead Swede who was really a "nice guy," but who the hell the person was who Benny called "Chief."

That was one of the things she didn't know. The other things she didn't know were what Benny did for a living, who his friends and connections were, who anybody was except his coterie of henchmen. She came to Benny when he wanted her, left when he said, "split," and listened to nothing that was said in her presence. If they hadn't tried to hurt me in Benny's study this night, she wouldn't have heard or seen a thing. But she couldn't stand people getting hurt.

And now look what she'd done. Now she didn't know if Benny'd ever speak to her again. If she hadn't interfered, Jan would still be alive, Benny wouldn't have been pistol-whipped. Oh, Benny was going to be awful mad at her. Maybe he wouldn't like her anymore.

I told her that might well be the least of her worries. "Benny's not only going to resent your spoiling his plans," I said, "he's not going to like your going off with me and talking to me."

"But you made me go with you. That wasn't my fault."

"He's not going to like it, all the same."

"And as for talking—I can't tell you anything. I don't know anything." She shrugged. "I'll tell him I didn't tell you anything."

"He might not believe you."

"Benny knows he can trust me."

I asked her about friends and relatives, people who would look out for her. She didn't have any—at least, any who could or would do her any real good. If Benny wanted to step on her, there wasn't anyone to stop him.

"But he wouldn't do that," she told me. "You don't have to worry."

"I do worry."

"Benny's a sweet guy, honest."

I took out a pen and wrote a phone number on her cocktail napkin. "The time may come when you'll change your mind," I told her. "If Benny or anybody else ever gives you trouble, you call this number and leave your name. Okay?"

She accepted it, but clearly thought me more

melodramatic than was necessary. "This your number?"

"No."

"I'd rather have your number." She looked at me. "Hey, I don't even know your name."

"Henry Marvin," I said, "and my number's private. This is how to reach me, but it's for emergency only. Call it and leave your name." I took the napkin back and wrote "S.O.S." over the number.

"All right, Mr. Marvin," she said slowly, tucking the napkin in her sash alongside her compact and whatever. She rose a little unsteadily and excused herself to go to the ladies' again.

I gave her fifteen minutes, then checked. As I expected, she'd gone out the back way so I couldn't follow her home. It seemed to me, falling for that old dodge was the easiest way to get rid of her.

I paid the check, climbed into a phone booth in the lobby and dialed the number I'd written on Lizabeth's napkin. It was Jack McGuire who answered, of course, and he picked up, yawning, on the second ring. I told him I was checking in, that I was still alive and all was well—more or less.

"If you're alive and well, what're you calling for at this hour? Did you think worry would spoil my sleep?"

"Not really."

"It's guilt, then. You've been doing something you don't think will help you get through the gates of heaven!"

I said, "I can tell you I've decided why I'm an unbeliever. It's because I don't think I'd do very well if I had to face a judgment day."

"You're going to face it whether you believe in it or not. We're all responsible for our actions in this world, my friend."

"I take responsibility. The buck stops here."

"If you recognize that, then you must recognize there's going to be a reckoning someday, somewhere, somehow. Otherwise the buck stops nowhere."

"Okay, Preach. What I'm calling about is to say that not everything came up roses tonight. There's a girl who I think is in trouble. She may need my help sometime. You follow me?"

"No."

"The long and short of it is, her name is Lizabeth Lynch. I gave her your phone number."

"Whose help did you say she's going to need?"

"My help. But I can't tell her who I am. The point is, if you or Mrs. Honeywell ever get called by someone with that name, get to me with the message as fast as you can. You got it?"

Jack sighed. "I got it. I just have one question. Why is it you heathens pick on us Catholics?"

IT WAS PUSHING TWO O'CLOCK when I drove the heap up the grade to my condo. I'd left Louie's Caddy over by Sylvia Rekkart's and felt more comfortable coming home behind the wheel of my own car.

That is, up until I nosed in beside the garage that's under my stairs. A strange car was in the next slot. It didn't belong to any of the neighbors and certainly not to the apartment next door, which was temporarily vacant.

So what of it? Somebody was having guests. It's nothing to get excited about, except that I excite easy.

I got out of my car slowly. Everything was dark. The nearest light was the streetlight down at the end of the grade, hidden behind the jutting forms of other condos.

I put my hand on the hood of the other car. It was warm. The car had only recently arrived, but there wasn't a light in any of the windows. Well, there are explanations for that, let's face it, but I didn't buy the easy ones. You don't live as long as I have in my line of work if you assume there's an innocent explanation for everything that's out of whack. Right now the same antennae that signaled, "Strange car," when I pulled in beside it were signaling, "You're it," when I found the hood still warm.

Why should I be it? The only dangerous work I was involved in was the protection racket, and I'd assumed a false identity. Nobody knew who I was. Nobody was after me. Go up the stairs and get to bed.

Like hell!

I didn't close my door. I got out my gun, and the adrenaline was pumping; I was manufacturing a lot of it tonight. I ducked low and went around my condo complex, through the narrow separating alley and into the woods on the back side. I moved slowly and quietly, feeling my way in the dark. Maybe I was a damned fool, but I didn't think so. I felt pretty damned smart, if you really want to know.

I circled through the woods, keeping well back, until the dome light inside my car came into view. Now I saw it through the stairs that climb to my storm porch. The way looked clear, but my antennae still said, "You're it."

There was one way to find out. I picked up a handful of stones and gravel, edged in to the side of the building out of sight of the stairs and crept to the corner. I took a breath, stepped into the open and let fly the fistful of stones at the doorway to the storm porch. I mean, I was fastball pitching from the stretch position.

Then I ducked back.

Good thing, too. There was a yelp of pain, then three thumping sounds, one after the other, all mingled with whistling, thudding noises. Those were bullets, coming out of a silencer, coming out of my doorway. Big bullets!

I poked my gun and one eye around the corner, and damned if a flashlight didn't go on up there in the entry. The assassin wanted to assess the damage. And, of course, the sweeping beam caught the part of me that showed.

I fired two fast shots at the light, jumped back to safety and dropped to one knee. The trouble was, being right-handed, I had to expose my whole body to fire around the corner. I took a chance, sticking head, shoulders and gun out from the new level, and let off another shot. He'd dropped the light and it was only a glow on the floor, so all I could do was fire at the center of the doorway and retreat.

I heard a grunt and a cough, then a thump. It made me think I'd scored, but there's an old trick called "playing possum." His flashlight was out of it, though, so I took a chance, came out from cover and let loose another quick shot.

It was wasted. What I saw as I let the shot go was a heavy form starting to roll down the steps. My slug went into the middle of it, but someone falling downstairs the way he was doesn't need any more bullets.

I ducked back by instinct, looked out again the next instant, and watched as the lumbering figure bumped and rolled and fell off the side of the steps to the ground.

I was over him before he came to rest, keeping one eye on the doorway above. It was obviously a one-man ambush, for two assassins wouldn't box themselves into the same corner, but you never can tell. It's even easier to underestimate stupidity than intelligence.

But it was safe. The guy was a loner. And he was very dead. In fact, when I brought his flashlight down and looked him over with it, I found I'd fired four shots and hit him four times. That's not bad for blind panic.

A light appeared in the condo across the way, but nobody came out. I didn't care if they did or didn't. I shone my light on the assassin's features and his clothes. The features weren't of anybody I remembered seeing before. The clothes were on the flashy side, the shoes were expensive. His gun, which he'd dropped on the floor with his flashlight, was a .38 revolver-cum-silencer. He was a paid killer trying to earn his keep.

Which meant somebody wanted me put out of the way. But I was only a sweet, innocent private detective minding his own business, trying to make friends, not enemies, right up till this afternoon. And any enemies I'd made since then thought I was somebody named Henry Marvin. At least, that's what they were supposed to think.

So what was this all about?

I went through the dead man's pockets, but there was nothing in them that meant anything. I located his wallet, which was slippery with blood, and took that and his flashlight and gun into the condo with me.

I turned on the light in the kitchen, put the gun and flash on the table, washed off the wallet and then went through it carefully.

There was no identification, of course. There was some money—enough for cab fare and not much more. The only other thing was a cropped photograph of me.

Never mind what he didn't have; that picture was worth the price of admission. It had been taken about ten years ago and showed me looking young and innocent and wet behind the ears, grinning like the kind of moron who believes love, not money, makes the world go around. The picture revealed only my head and part of my shoulders. My hair was tousled and my shoulders were bare. The background was sky. I might have been in a bathing suit. The sharpness of the shadows and the bare shoulders gave it the look of summer. It could have been at the beach.

I suspected others had been in the picture with me. The fuzziness made it look like an enlargement from a snap, so I would only have occupied a small part. Also, the cropping took off part of my left shoulder but left the whole of the right, so that I wasn't centered.

But who, when and why? If it was a beach scene, there would have been others with me—at least a girl, maybe boys and girls, maybe boys. I never went alone.

And this picture had been cut from a larger picture and given to the assassin as identification by the person who wanted me eliminated. That somebody didn't have any more recent pictures, but that somebody *did* have that picture. So whom might I have gone to the beach with back around age twenty? Good God, there were so many I couldn't begin to think.

Well, that was neither here nor there. There were other things that took priority. Like it or not, one can't leave dead bodies lying around. The police would have to be called, and I'd be up the rest of the night answering questions. Well, what I did when I came home here would be their business. What I'd been doing the rest of the time was my own. That they could jump in the lake for.

I picked up the kitchen phone and dialed Emergency.

14

A DETECTIVE NAMED LASKY was in charge. He'd been catching the last time I had trouble, but he'd been outranked and kept still. Tonight he was top dog, feeling his oats and eager to show me how tough he was. First he wanted to know what there was about my place that attracted bullets. I said I wished I knew. He decided *he* knew and accused me of being up to my earlobes in vice and villainy, and of double-crossing the gang to boot. From that theory he deduced I knew who'd set me up for the shooting. I said I knew nothing. That didn't stop him.

"You don't fool me, you sons of bitches," he snarled. "You wouldn't tell the cops anything on your deathbed. You hoods all think you're going to settle your own wars."

There finally comes a time. This was it. I stuck a finger in his sternum and said, "Watch what names you call me, Chester. I get angry easy."

He brushed my hand away with a swipe. "My name ain't Chester."

"And mine ain't 'hood.'"

Tom Burwell, a massive cop standing beside us

in my foyer, grabbed my arm and backed me up a step soothingly. "Now, Simon, don't get sore so easy. You know Detective Lasky don't mean nothing."

"I don't know what Detective Lasky means," I snapped. "I'll tell you what I mean, though. I got shot at three times by that dead son of a bitch out there—"

"Yeah, but you got even with him. Better than even."

"I said I got shot at three times. I could've been lying where he is. That kind of thing doesn't sit well with me at two o'clock in the morning. It makes me nervous. It makes me short-tempered. So when some detective claims I know who sent that hit man but I don't want to tell, he's got egg whites for brains." I turned to Lasky. "That's his wallet and stuff on the kitchen table. That's his car outside. Go detect if you're so smart. They'll tell you more about him than I can."

Lasky was hard-nosed. "Somebody tries to ambush you, but you don't know anything about it. You aren't expecting anything at all. But it turns out you ambush the ambusher. Just a happy-accident kind of thing, right?"

"I told you the car didn't belong here and the hood was warm."

"And that tells you somebody's laying for you, huh? Where do you get off reading that kind of interpretation into it?"

"I lead that kind of life."

He didn't like it, but I wouldn't melt and there

wasn't much he could do. At least he had the victim and the victim's car and the victim's wallet and other belongings—all except for the cropped photograph of me. I kept that in my own wallet.

They departed finally, about half-past three, and Lasky didn't even offer to leave a man on guard in case some backup assassins came prowling.

That was all right. I wouldn't have let him stay anyway. It was enough with the locks on my doors and my gun. Lasky wanted to impound my gun, but that would have meant my lawyer coming to the rescue, and judges and court orders and the works, and he'd have been there till noon trying to make it stick. Besides, one thing he could appreciate was my need for it. He wore one himself, and he knew.

I SLEPT WHAT SLEEP I COULD and got up with the alarm at seven, bracing for a new day. I didn't face it in the best of moods, either. I was tired, I was cross, and some of the adrenaline was still poisoning my system. Also, there was the question of who'd be trying to shoot me next, where and when, and that was raising hell with my digestion. Ignorance ain't no kind of bliss, no matter what the poet says.

But life goes on, and I did have to function. There were captives to feed and an office to get to. A number of people relied on me for one thing or another.

I packed a lunch basket with hard-boiled eggs,

cereal and milk, stuffing in bowls, spoons and napkins for ballast. Then I trekked out to my barnyard zoo to see what my pet hyenas wanted to laugh about. I also thought I'd twist their arms while they ate to see what tips they could give me as to who had hired the assassin. I didn't figure Lasky would get far along that yellow brick road.

It was a raw windy day with the threat of a rain that would chill more than snow. The sky was the color of slate, the telephone wires whined, and the weather reports spelled B-L-E-A-K. The effect was depressing. I was in a mood to be depressed.

I rode the main drags, and traffic gnawed at my heels and built in front. Then I hit the farmhouse road and was all alone. It was almost as bad. I felt pressured to hurry, as if the sky were falling, but I didn't know why. Yes, I did. It was the assassin complex. I didn't know what would happen next.

Then I was pulling into the clearing, and the house stood quiet and untouched, looking reassuringly as I had left it. Anybody passing by would think it empty. It had that empty look. In fact, it reeked of emptiness.

I parked and studied its hard shabby outlines. I wished my head felt better. I wished my ribs didn't ache. I wished my stomach would decide what position to take.

Was that a broken window? Wasn't there a chunk of pane missing near the catch?

I stared. Had it been like that before? I couldn't

remember: but that meant it hadn't, for I notice such things.

I got out of the car with my gun in my hand. I used the car as a shield until I could duck to the window. The wind crispened, but it was the only sound. I peeked through the glass, but the inside was too dim.

I slipped quietly to the door, held the gun muzzle up and tried the knob. It moved readily.

I pushed a little. The door wasn't locked. But I had locked it.

So what do you do? You fish or cut bait. I kicked the door wide and went in, gun level, going for anything that moved.

There wasn't anything *to* move.

There was no Richie, no Louie, no sign of the ropes that had bound them, no sign they'd ever been there.

It was nothing but an empty house.

If you think I'd been feeling punk before, that was nothing. This was the kind of feeling where you stare in disbelief and tell yourself that if you stare hard enough, you'll see them.

But you don't. And then you pull yourself together and realize you're wasting time, you ought to be doing something—like, maybe, *detecting*.

I went to the broken window. It had been smashed from the outside to reach the lock. It was the means of entry, and one or more people had freed my prisoners and taken them out the door.

It was a simple enough rescue. A child could have done it. But who knew where the prisoners were? And how?

I tried to gather my wits. Those problems came later. The point was, Richie Zullo and Louie the Greek were loose. And what would they do with their newfound freedom? If I could make any sense out of this crazy charade, they'd make tracks for Rafe's store and string mom and pop up by their thumbs until they revealed that Simon Kaye was the supercluck who had promised them nirvana.

I didn't lock the door; I didn't do anything but jump back into the car, shift gears and scream into a tight left-hand circle heading out the drive. I didn't know how long Richie and Louie had been free. I didn't know how much of a head start they'd had.

I didn't go to the Rafes' after all. The eight-thirty news on the car radio changed my mind. "Word is just in," the announcer said, and there was the rustle of someone picking up a flash bulletin. "The bodies of two murder victims have just been discovered in the trunk of a stolen car abandoned in a local service station. The car, a late-model Pontiac, was found by filling-station attendants dripping blood from its trunk in front of the service doors when they opened the station at half-past six this morning. Identification of the bodies by articles in their clothing has since been confirmed by police. The two victims, slain gangland style with multiple bullet wounds in the head, are Richard Zullo of 241 Leftward Place, and Louis Bustoni of the Belmore Vista apartments, who was known to intimates as Louie the Greek. Motive for their slaying remains a mystery."

That threw a new wrinkle into the web. Louie and Richie had been tracked down not by rescuers but by executioners.

A lot of things were bubbling in the stewpot, and I didn't have a glimmer as to the recipe.

When I got to the office I began to find out.

15

EILEEN HAD ARRIVED at the office just ahead of me and was standing, hands on hips, in the middle of a shambles. The whole place had been ransacked, files tumbled, chairs overturned, papers scattered. Wastebaskets were upside down and the waiting-room magazines had been thrown against the walls to see what would fall out. From the extent of the chaos, our cleaning woman would want a raise.

When I found her, Eileen was still in shock. There are three stages of response to such vandalism. The first is disbelief. That's replaced by fury at the invasion of privacy. Even if nothing has been stolen, the fury is there. Lastly there develops the element of fear—that someone wants to do you harm and will be back.

Eileen went from step one to step three, bypassing step two. The desecration didn't bother her. The motive did. "Simon," she said when she heard me behind her, "what is all this?"

"Breaking and entering, from the looks of things."

She turned. "Simon, I'm scared."

"Spoken like a true women's libber," I answered, trying to sound like a rock-hard palace guard. But to tell the truth, I was scared, too.

She came close to me. "What is it? What're you into?"

"Everybody gets burgled," I said, but she gave me no heed. You can't con that girl with any trick I've ever tried.

"Why did they do this to you?" she said. "Does it have to do with that house you rented?"

Up till that moment, all the shambles meant to me was that somebody had broken into the office for God only knew what reason. Now Eileen had given me a clue.

I grabbed her by the arms, almost lifting her off the ground. "That lease! Where'd you put it?"

Her green eyes widened, sparkled and dimmed. "Wait a minute." She pulled away to think, and her cleavage heaved. (I wish to hell she'd wear Mother Hubbards if we're going to deal with serious matters.) She said, "It was on my desk. I left it on my desk in a folder."

"You showed it to me. You asked about it!"

She nodded. "It was new in the files. I showed it, and I left it out." She gave me an arch look. "I wanted to memorize the address."

"It makes a lousy love nest, if that's what you're thinking."

Her look grew far more arch. "What makes you think you know what I'm thinking?"

"You left it on the desk?"

"In the 'unfiled' folder."

"There's nothing on your desk now."

"It's probably on the floor."

"Let's find it."

"You don't think they'd take that, do you?"

"I want to find out."

"But it would've been the first thing the burglars would have found. If that's what they wanted, they wouldn't have gone through all the rest of the files."

"Who says they did?"

Eileen gestured at the mess. "What more evidence do you need?"

"Throwing drawers of stuff around a room doesn't mean the stuff has been examined. Now help me hunt for that lease. If it's here, that's one thing. If it isn't, that's another."

Eileen obeyed and started gathering up and going through papers. She said, "Which gets the gold star, finding it or not finding it?"

I said, "If we don't find it, I'm in the dark. If we do find it, I'm even more in the dark."

Eileen tackled the job aggressively. She said, "I'll bet if I worked for the CIA, I'd know a hell of a lot more about what's going on than I do around here!"

Of course we didn't find it. The thieves had picked it up and gone to see what I was stashing in that particular little piece of real estate. And what they found were two members of their fraternity: Richard Zullo and Louie the Greek. And because Richie and Louie were responsible for the way things had come about, and because things had turned out very bad—at least from the standpoint of Mr. Big—Richie and Louie were dispensed with as unwanted members of the fraternity.

And the moral of that is: if you want to survive in the jungle, you have to be the biggest. Your life span varies according to size.

I left Eileen to the task of cleaning up, and got out of there before she read any more of my mind. She knew I was in trouble, but she didn't know how deep. In fact, I was only just groping with the depths myself.

There was only one way to tie the pieces together: the Henry Marvin fake hadn't worked. Someone at Benny's party had recognized me, and I was no sooner out of his apartment than it was known who'd wracked up his bodyguards and run off with his girl.

That's why the assassin was staking out *my* condo, that's why burglars ransacked *my* office. That's how Richie and Louie came to be found and made to talk.

But it wasn't Benny who put those wheels in motion. He wasn't in shape and he didn't have the manpower. It was Mr. Big who was quarterbacking the game. Benny was only mending his face and talking with the cops.

Mr. Big was the guy I wanted to find. Instead he'd found me! It was a handicap I wouldn't want to list on a life-insurance application.

Tracking him down wasn't going to be easy

now. Benny was my contact, but I had the feeling I wasn't going to get close to Benny for a while. In fact, I was the one who needed to hide, not Benny.

The long and short of it was, I was in over my head and if I didn't get some help I wasn't going to be around very long. More to the point, the Rafes were in the same kind of spot. And I'd put them there.

Something had to be done about that. I climbed into my heap and headed their way.

16

MOM WAS BEHIND THE CIGAR COUNTER handing three packs of weeds to a female chimney who spilled ashes down a front so fat she could have joined the circus. Doria was stuffing an ice-cream cone for a tad who had to stand on the foot rail to see over the counter. Pop was replenishing the magazine racks, and all of them looked sober and wan until I walked in. The reason for their gray unease was that they'd given me the keys to the castle yesterday afternoon and I'd walked off with the ogre and that was the last they'd heard. What act two would bring, they wouldn't know until they saw which of us walked through their door next—him or me.

It was I, and the sun came out. Pop came to shake my hand, Doria gave me a kiss right on the mouth, and mama came clucking over before she'd even banked the fat woman's change in the register. She looked at me like I was something holy.

It made me feel lousy. They thought, because I was the one who returned, that the game was won and they were free from fear from now on.

Instead I had to warn them to be careful, that I couldn't protect them, that I didn't know what might happen.

I was almost brusque getting Doria into a corner, and mom and pop grew apprehensive again. It seemed incredible, after all that had happened, that this was only the morning after I'd whisked Richie Zullo out of their store and given them a reprieve. Now Richie was dead and I was wondering whether it was a reprieve or the calm before the storm.

Doria's injured eyes were wide, and she had both hands on my sleeves. Damn those eyes. You'd do anything to get the fear out of them. Not almost anything, but anything.

But I had nothing to work with. I was more scared than she. I'd jumped in with both feet and set a cyclone going. What the hell did I think, that Super-Simon-to-the-rescue would end the terror that afflicted her family? "Don't sell yourself on the streets, dear lady; Sir Lancelot will save you from a fate worse than death. Name your dragons and I will slay them!"

And now there I was in the corner of her store, with Doria almost up against me, gazing haplessly into my face. And what was I to say? "Beware! The Slime Monster is going to devour you!" Or maybe I should tell Doria that she made a big mistake, that she should never have come to me, that it was like asking an apprentice plumber to fix Grand Coulee Dam.

That would do no good. I couldn't let her down. I had to get some help.

"Listen," I said, "things are in flux. I can't tell what's going to happen. One thing I have to know. Where can I get hold of Archie Fallon?"

She sucked in her breath at mention of his name, and her eyes hardened. You wouldn't believe, having gazed into those soft, warm, melting glimmers, how stonelike they could become. They could drive you to a monastery.

She shook her head. "No," she whispered. "Not Archie. I told you. I'd rather go to the streets—"

"Not you," I said. "Me!" I seized her arms. "I want to talk to him."

A corner of her mouth twisted. "Why? You know what he's like."

"I know what he's like," I answered. "But he can help."

"How? Why?"

Clever, clever Doria. There were many "hows," there were almost no "whys."

"He loves you," I said.

"He wants me," she answered.

"And I hope he'll want to save you."

"But what can he do?" she asked me. "What would he do if he could?"

"He can give me some names," I answered, speaking with an assurance that I hoped would convince.

"What names? What would he know?"

"Listen," I said, grasping her more firmly.

"He's big in real estate, right? He's going to know who's after what and why. He's going to know what's valuable."

"So?"

"So your folks have had the protection money on their store raised and raised until they can't pay it anymore. But nobody else has had his ante raised. There's a reason, then. Somebody wants to drive your folks out of business."

She nodded. "That's obvious."

"So what are the reasons for the big shot driving your folks out of business? He's not going to want to take over the store; it's not that profitable. The logical answer, therefore, is that somebody wants to get hold of this piece of property cheap. It's not the store, it's the land the store occupies. It's my guess somebody is trying to buy up the whole area."

Doria's eyes widened. "Maybe Archie himself?"

"That would be interesting."

"That would mean he—he's—in with the people in the protection racket?"

"That sounds like Archie, even including selling out the girl he loves for a fast buck." I shrugged. "But that's neither here nor there. I want to know how to get to him."

"He's in the phone book."

"His real-estate firm is in the phone book. I want the private number and the personal address. I want what you've got."

"He won't do anything for you, Simon. You've said so yourself. You knew him when."

"But he might do something for you. You're in danger and I can't protect you. I'm not big enough and strong enough. Archie is. If he cares for you at all. . . ."

Doria paled. My seven-league boots had turned to feet of clay. I'm not happy to lose face with the beholden, but first things first. I wasn't Lancelot, and Archie certainly wasn't King Arthur. Maybe, though, he could be Merlin. That was what we both had to count on, and she told me what I had to know.

17

THE LAST PERSON IN THE WORLD I wanted to see was Archie Fallon. Our paths hadn't crossed in ten years, and I would have liked it to be forever. He'd come back to the old neighborhood to strut his stuff and let the younger crowd see what a big shot he'd become. He was twenty-seven then, and sported diamond rings on two pinkies, Italian-leather shoes, three-hundred-dollar double-breasted suits and gross painted ties that almost glowed in the dark. He also sported a paunch that stuck a foot out over his belt. He was big there, too.

That time he'd spoken to me, the inevitable sneer in his voice. But I hadn't spoken to him. I thought I never would again. But time and tides play funny tricks. Now I was going to him, hat in hand. I wasn't going only to speak to him, I was going to beg from him.

His house was a Victorian mansion near the center of town. Originally it had been built for and inhabited by the superrich. When that era faded, the only way the house could remain standing was by the estate converting it into a combination museum and public library.

That was a losing proposition, too, and was being phased out when Archie was making his pile. From what Doria told me, he took it over, and the hulking monstrosity was what he now quietly called home. It was one of those ploys carried out so secretly I didn't know it had happened, and I'm in a business that is up on the local news. Archie Fallon moved a lot, mostly up the ladder, mostly without a sound being made. Now I went to his home address and found that his living room was where I used to read Hardy Boys mysteries and once, almost under the nose of the librarian, unscrewed the screen and crawled through a ventilation tunnel on a dare from Jack McGuire.

I played my approach to Archie with awkward naiveté. It was the kind of approach he would appreciate—no phone call, no appointment, just an arrival on the front porch, ringing the doorbell and standing there with all the innocence of the Avon Lady at a house of ill-repute.

I had to leave my name with the butler and wait in the open air, but it wasn't long. I didn't think it would be. Then I was ushered through carpeted hallways walled with mahogany panels, lighted with too dim sconces, into a plush rear office that was very different from the rest of the house. The furnishings were just as ornate and the carpeting as elegant, but there were blue steel cabinets, a copying machine, a metal water cooler, and a coffee urn on a steel table that said the fun and games ended outside. In this room the brains crackled and ideas had a stench. I could almost smell the sulfur and brimstone.

And it was behind an ornamental desk almost as mammoth as the man himself that Archie Fallon sat. He'd been obese at twenty-seven; he was a behemoth at thirty-seven. He made the house look small. His cheeks and jowls jiggled, his eyebrows were arches over piglet eyes, and that smile of his that had always looked like the first crescent of a new moon tilted the ends of his mouth like a Dali mustache.

He was pleased to see me. He was more pleased than you would ever know. It didn't show in his manner, it showed in his smile. There was that inner glee that bespeaks custody of the brass ring.

"Well, we meet again," he said without trying to get up, without moving, really, and without gesturing at a chair. Of course he didn't offer me his hand. We both knew I'd take it in my teeth.

"You're doing well," I said, looking around the room and sitting in an unbidden chair. I looked around again, at the expensive paintings, the expensive decor, his expensive waistline. "Better than the widows and orphans."

He wasn't put off by that. "Better than private detectives," he added, giving me the glint of a gold tooth.

"Real estate pays well," I said.

"It tells you where the bargains are." He waved a hand. "The real key is promotion. Some people will tell you the way to make money is to buy and sell—be the middleman. Buy cheap and sell dear." He shook his head. "The real key to wealth is to promote. Buy, *develop* and then sell. You buy the apple off the tree, you polish it and make it shine and then you sell it."

"That's how to make good, huh? That's how you got to this desk in this house?"

He nodded. "That's the ticket. Honest labor. I've learned in life that honest labor pays off. In the real-estate business I'm a developer. I buy land. I put stores and houses on that land. Then I sell that land to people who want to own stores and live in houses. I convert a useless tract of ground into a desirable commodity. The rewards are great!" He gestured at the paintings and other nearby rewards. "And it's honest and aboveboard. That's the real pleasure of it all."

I said, "I can remember when you didn't put much stock in honesty."

"When I was young and innocent. In those days I thought the fast buck had to be a crooked buck. I've since learned different. The fast buck goes to the smart guy, not the crook. Let me tell you something. The meek don't inherit the earth. The smart guys inherit the earth."

I said, "A lot of smart guys I've known have inherited six feet of it—on top of their coffins."

Archie Fallon laughed. This was probably the first time I'd ever amused him. "Now you're talking about crooks again. You aren't listening to me, Simon. I've just been telling you it pays to be honest. Because the honest man can make just as much money as the dishonest man, but he can do it with one big plus in his favor." He waited for me to ask the proper question.

Naturally, I asked it. "What's the big plus?"

Archie chuckled. He'd had a girlish laugh when he was fourteen, trying to wrestle ten-year-old girls. It had a harshness to it when he was twenty-seven, wearing his diamond-studded rings and supplying the women of his fancy with Cadillacs.

Now his chuckle had a richness to it, the confident purr of the man who'd bought his way to the top, who knew what it took and had what it took.

Now he could preach to me on the value of virtue. It wasn't enough that I had to sit with my hat in my hand; I had to sit at his feet, as well. I can tell you, I wouldn't have done it for anyone but Doria.

Eventually his glee subsided enough for him to arch his eyebrows. Some people can arch one. He did both. "Well, I'm sure you haven't come here to hear me lecture on the path to success. Success has quite obviously never been one of your goals in life. You must be here for another reason."

I allowed as how I'd come to him for information, but not quite the information he'd been dispensing, much as I'd learned from listening.

"Well," he said, leaning back in his chair, "some of us have it and some of us don't."

"That's true," I said, and we nodded in agreement. Except that I was looking at his waistline and he thought I was looking at his bank account.

"And what's the information you're after?" he asked.

His tone was generous, that of the squire encouraging a serf. It didn't mean he had any intention of giving it to me. It only meant he wanted to find out where his power lay.

I crossed my fingers and set sail. "You're up on things," I said. "You're in the know. You didn't get to your position of eminence without being on the inside of what's going on."

His eyes grew hooded. "Well?"

"Who runs the protection racket in this city?"

The eyes betrayed nothing. "What protection racket?"

"Are you going to pretend you don't know what the hell rackets operate in this town?" I couldn't help laughing.

His nose lifted a little. "I'm not going to pretend there's no crime in this town," he said. "I'm only going to tell you I'm not involved in it."

"I didn't say you were. I said I want to know who is."

"And if I knew, do you think I'd tell you?"

"If it would help somebody you cared about very much."

Was there a trace of a smile around his lips? "Who're you talking about?" The eyes were narrow, but the smile was definitely there.

He knew whom I meant, all right. I could read it in his eyes. He knew what my whole pitch was about. He just wanted to hear me say it. So that's what he wanted? That's what he'd get.

"I'm talking about Doria Rafe," I answered. "She's in trouble, and I think you know it."

"Really?" he said, arching those eyebrows. "Doria's in trouble? I'm surprised she hasn't let me know."

"She hasn't told you?" He was lying, of course. She'd told him first thing and learned his price. That's why I was there—to whittle him down a little.

"Perhaps she's reluctant to share her problems with me," he said, and an unpleasant look came into his eyes. "But she turns to you? Is that my understanding?"

"She's in trouble—or rather, her folks are in trouble."

"And she turns to you?" He laughed harshly. "Tell me, Simon, what does she think you can do for her?"

"Go to bat, I suppose."

He laughed again, this time more silkily, but the ugliness was deeper. "Quite obviously she never heard of a certain young woman we both used to know. Wouldn't you agree?"

"I don't know what you're talking about."

"Of course you do. Her name was Moira—a lovely name, don't you think? Moira Stevenson. Don't tell me you don't remember Moira Stevenson."

He was going to do everything he could to hurt. I gritted my teeth. "Yes, I remember Moira Stevenson."

"She was a lovely girl, wasn't she?"

"Yes."

He didn't like my curt dismissal of the subject. "Describe her to me, Simon," he purred. "Tell me what she looked like."

"What for? You know what she looked like."

"I want to hear you tell it." He gave me that half-moon grin. "You want something from me, I want something from you. I want to hear you describe her."

"Blond hair, dark eyes. Oval face."

Archie held up a hand. "Not so fast. You're not going to sell real estate that way. Make me want her."

"What the hell for?"

His eyes got hard. "Because I say so."

I took a breath. "Dark brown eyes, dark brows and lashes. Blond hair, shoulder length. Dirty blond, really—"

"Sun-kissed blond," Archie interrupted.

I laughed. "Sun-kissed? She'd have exploded. She always called herself 'dirty blond.'"

Archie, surprisingly, turned red with fury. He snatched up a studio portrait from his desk and turned it my way. He'd have rammed it into my face if he could have reached. "Take a look!" he snarled. "Do you call *that* 'dirty blond'?"

It was of Moira, head and shoulders, tinted and airbrushed until all the life was gone and only an angel remained.

I knew enough to shake my head. "No, you're right. She's a sun-kissed blonde."

He pulled the picture back and reset it facing him. There were a lot of other things on the desk, but that was the only photo.

He took a couple of heavy breaths to reestablish both his calm and his ascendancy. He lifted his gaze from the photograph. "What about her figure?"

"Good figure."

"You can do better than that."

"What the hell do you want," I said testily, "her measurements? You know them better than I do."

His eyes were black with hate. "Tell me about her figure!"

"She had a figure that would give the statue of David an erection."

He liked that. I thought he would. Some of the tension left him. "How old was she?"

"Twenty-two."

"How old were you?"

"Twenty."

"Did you ask her to marry you?"

"I did."

Archie purred some more. "What did she say?"

"She said no."

"Did she give you a reason?"

"She said I was too young."

Half his grin remained, but there was something behind his eyes. "I think she gave you another reason."

"She said she was going to marry someone else."

"I think she only said she was *hoping* to marry someone else."

"Hoping to marry someone else."

"Why?"

He was going to drag it out of me, and let me tell you, I was hurting. Moira was as nice a kid as you could want to meet. So she had a couple of years on me; we hit it off. I was young, but not really foolish. I thought I had a chance.

I said to Archie, "She told me she was in love with this other person."

"You can mention his name; I don't mind."

"She said she was in love with you."

His laugh was gloating. "Hard to get the words out, isn't it? It galls you, doesn't it?" His voice grew ugly again. "Just because you're big and strong, with a good physique, you think all the girls should kiss your ass. You think physique's all that matters to a girl. You think that's all it takes. So you can't stand losing out to someone who isn't built as well as you are, who isn't as big and strong as you are. It galls you that someone who isn't as macho as you are can beat you out. It galls you that someone like me can make it with a girl when you can't. It galls you that they want something in a man that you can't give. You didn't like being called 'too young,' did you? You didn't like her marrying a mature man instead of a virile one."

He sneered at me then. "It galled you thinking of us in bed together, didn't it? You'd always hated me, and I beat you out in the one area where you thought you were invincible. Sure, I could make money when you couldn't. You figured you could attract the girls and that would compensate. But I beat you there, too, didn't I?"

"Yes, you did."

There was no denying it. Nor was there any point in crowing because his big happy marriage hadn't lasted two months. Moira had died in a tragic accident less than a week after they returned from the honeymoon. It wasn't his fault. He'd been in Europe on business when it happened, and I'd heard it hit him hard. So if he wanted to rub it into me that he'd won her and I hadn't, I could sit there and take it. If she'd said yes to me, who knows what course my life might have taken? But that was water long over the dam, and I really hadn't thought of Moira in half a dozen years. Even when Doria mentioned the name Archie Fallon to me, I hadn't thought of Moira. Never mind the marriage; they didn't go together.

"And now," Archie said, sitting back and rubbing his palms together, but with no smile on his face, "what are you trying to do, beat me out again?"

"Me?"

"That's right, with Doria."

I didn't want him holding that against her. "Hell, no," I said. "I don't even know the girl."

"You don't know her, but you're here on her behalf. You amuse me, Kaye."

I walked that one around two or three times,

trying to make him understand I was a friend of the family with no stake in the outcome. Let's not say he believed it, but let's say he was willing to move on to other subjects. He tilted his chair back, watching me like a snake, all the while he rubbed his palms together and tried to produce his half-moon smile.

There was no point in jousting with him. He was too smart to fool, and he probably knew twice as much about the matter as I did. I'd only dig Doria and her folks a coffin pit if I tried to distort the truth. The family, I told Archie, was being deliberately forced out of business by the boss of the protection racket. The bite on them was taking big jumps while all the other shop-keepers were being victimized at the same old rate.

This meant a vendetta by the protection boss against the Rafe family, or it meant he wanted to buy up their property cheap. Either way they needed help.

"So they go to you, the private detective?" He couldn't keep the sneer out of his voice.

"And I'm coming to you."

"What makes you think I could help you if I wanted to?"

"I figure you can give me the name of Mr. Big in the protection racket."

"Guess again. I'm in real estate."

"I figure if you don't know, you can find out."

"If I could, do you think I'd tell you?" He laughed with that same mirthless ugly sound.

"You wantta beat me out with Doria, huh? And you want me to help you?"

"To tell the truth, I'm trying to get an angle on what's going on. What does the guy want?"

"Ask him. Don't come to me."

"I'm thinking—if it's not a desire to crush the Rafe family, and they don't know why Mr. Big should want to do that—then the guy must want the property. For certain reasons, it's a prime piece of real estate."

Archie snorted. "No wonder you're a poverty-stricken cluck, scrounging a meager living in the detective racket. You don't have enough brains to be a detective. A prime piece of real estate? That neighborhood was the pits when you and I were growing up down there. It's worse now than it was then. Values in that part of town are going down, not up. If you had ten cents' worth of brains inside that thick head of yours, you'd know the Rafes are damned lucky to make a living out of that place. And if you know them, you know it isn't that much of a living." He gestured past me in the direction of the front of his house. "You could put their whole damned store in my living room." He pointed his finger in my direction. "That's the difference between you and me, sucker. I make money because I know what to invest in. You don't because you don't know. If you think there's any value in any of the properties down there, all I can say is, stay out of the real-estate business. You'll lose your shirt."

Archie was great with sermons this day. He had

his archenemy as a captive audience and he couldn't let go. In fact, I hadn't realized until now how much of an archenemy I was. Sure, he'd beaten me out with Moira; that didn't make up for the bloody nose I gave him when I was seven. Nothing ever would.

Since I didn't reply to his assessment of me as a real-estate operator, he led with another question; another several questions. "So what the hell are you really here for?" he said angrily. "You think I'm going to tell you who runs the protection racket in this city? You think I'm going to tell you the name of the president of the United States? You think I'm going to tell you anything? You know better than that.

"So why are you here?" Archie Fallon waved an angry hand. "You think I'm stupider than you are. That's the real reason you're here. You think you can get something out of me free, for nothing." He shook his head and pointed at my head. "Dumb, dumb, dumb." He indicated his surroundings. "You think somebody dumber than you has all this while you live in a hovel and pride yourself on your brains?"

"You know I live in a hovel?"

Archie snorted. "I don't know how you live, but it's not so grand as this. I look at you and know that. I measure the quality of your clothes against mine. It tells me the quality of your living against mine."

"Is that why you let me in, so that you could contrast our life-styles?"

He shrugged. "I let you in because you amuse me."

"And Doria also amuses you?"

He didn't like that crack, and his brows clamped. "You came to me. I didn't tell you to. You're dirt, Simon Kaye. You're nothing. You'll never *be* anything. I've had enough of being reminded of you. State your business and get out."

I said, "My business is Doria Rafe's welfare. I came because I thought it was yours."

"Talk is cheap. Tell me what you want. Spell it out, schmuck."

"I want her folks left alone. That means no more protection money, no more bombs through their storefront."

Archie snorted. "And you think *I* can arrange that? You think I'm Mr. Wonderful?"

"That's right. I think you can. I think you know who and you know how. I think if *you* decide it will stop, it *will* stop."

"Then why does Doria go through a middleman? If *you* come to me, why doesn't *she* come to me? What's your cut?"

I said, "I should've remembered who I'm talking to. You *would* think that way. Doria came to me because she didn't know you could do anything for her. I *do* know."

That smile played with his lips. It was unpretty to watch.

He sat back in his chair and regarded me with interested eyes. I couldn't tell whether he was amused or calculating. He was very careful about his eyes.

"Let's suppose," he said, and gestured casually, "that I'm the Mr. Wonderful you think I am. Let's suppose I got where I am because I can make the impossible happen." The grin grew a little. "What kind of a price would you pay to have the impossible happen?"

"Are you talking about money?"

"Of course not. I don't need money and you don't have any. Quite obviously we're talking about the things money can't buy."

"Such as?"

"You want my terms? You want me to be forthright?"

"By all means."

"I want Doria to be my wife."

I had a feeling he was going to say that, just because he knew it was something I couldn't manage. "You've got to do better than that," I said.

He snorted. "How could I do better than Doria for my wife?"

I pointed a finger. "You've got a picture of another girl on your desk. She's the one you want, not Doria."

Archie laid the photo on its face. "She's dead," he said. "I'm alive."

"And you want to marry Doria?"

"You heard me."

"Then why don't you speak for yourself."

"Because I've got *you* to speak for me," he

said, "You're the virile one, the macho hero. Make a pitch, hero. Let's see how good you are." He lifted up the facedown photo and stared at Moira Stevenson Fallon's tinted image to remind me of my failure. "Yeah, Simon. Let's see how good you are."

WHEN I GOT OUTSIDE Archie Fallon's gingerbread palace, I spit on the sidewalk. It was the nearest I could come to taking a bath. But spitting didn't buy me any solutions. It didn't even make me feel better. I wondered enviously what it would be like to have money and power and be able to get what you wanted out of the world. That didn't make me feel better, either.

I drove back to the store, feeling as useless as a sponge in a dry-ice factory. Doria was up front, and I shook my head when I came in. She shrugged. It was what she expected. Pop tried to make me feel comfortable. "You look worried, son," he said. "It's all right. You did your best."

I said, "That's not what I'm worried about. I'm afraid the guys who run the protection racket will blame you for what I did."

He put a hand on my arm. "Forget it," he said. "I didn't have the money anyway. Whatever they do, they'd do whether you were in it or not. At least we fought 'em."

That didn't make me feel better, either.

The Rafes weren't my only worry. I stopped for lunch at a grease-and-gravy joint and called Jack McGuire to see if he'd been S.O.S.'d by Lizabeth Lynch. He was sitting down to corn fritters and crabmeat salad, he told me, and I wished he hadn't. I was having corned-beef hash and a poached egg. Mrs. Honeywell takes great care of Father Jack, let me tell you.

From his interest in describing his lunch, I knew he hadn't heard from Lizabeth. He confirmed the fact and when I didn't sound happy said, "What're you worrying for? No news is good news."

"In her case I'm not so sure. She might not have had the chance to call."

"And you don't know where she lives?"

"No, and she's not in the phone book, at least under that name."

"Don't sweat about it, Simon. She's probably all right."

"Let's hope."

Jack sighed. "Quite obviously she's deeper in trouble than you've been telling me. In fact, you haven't told me anything. Not hearing from her is as bad as hearing from her, do I have that straight?"

"Hell," I said, "I don't know. She's one of two broads I rubbed up against yesterday who belong to hoods. They shack up with these bums, knowing full well what they're about, knowing full well the rain may fall. So when it does, who ends up supplying the umbrella? I do! I should be sending her to you. You're the goddamn priest. I'm nothing but a heathen who doesn't pray, who takes the name of the Lord in vain and breaks all the commandments—most of them, anyway. How do I get into these spots?''

''Because you're a worrier. Worriers are even better than priests.''

''Go eat your corn fritters and crabmeat salad,'' I told him. ''I can get better advice from Ann Landers.''

THE CORNED-BEEF HASH was mostly potatoes and the egg was bathed in warm grease. It wouldn't have tasted good even if I hadn't known what Jack was eating, but I wasn't expecting this to be one of my better days.

I drove back to the office then to see if Eileen was putting it back together or had decided to take her vacation instead. She was there, and the place was in reasonably good shape. What hadn't been put away was at least stacked.

When she saw me she said, ''Just the man I've been waiting for,'' drew a bottle of brandy out of the bottom drawer of her desk, stood it on the top and went for paper cups from the water cooler.

I pointed at the bottle. ''Say, how long have you been stashing brandy—''

''They stole everything in your liquor file last night and I figured you'd need something to make you forget.''

''So you bought a new bottle of brandy—''

"And I've got it in *my* drawer because I haven't fixed your office yet, and if you saw that, it'd take more than one bottle to straighten you out."

"You bucking for sainthood?" I asked.

"No, just a raise."

"Sainthood's easier."

"I already know that," she said, pouring a half cup of brandy for me and a small amount for her. "I've been collecting your messages."

"And?"

We touched cups and I sipped the amber liquid. The brand wasn't familiar, but it was good stuff. I took another swallow.

"And," she said, draining her cup in unladylike fashion, "I need the drink more than you do."

"They must be interesting messages."

"They are." She gave me one. A client's check had bounced and he'd left town. "There goes next month's rent."

"Don't bet on it," I said. "You forget I'm a detective. It says so on my license."

"That's right. I keep thinking you're in real estate."

She was worried about the missing lease. I had another swallow of brandy. "What else?"

"Two reporters called, one from each paper. They want an interview about the man who tried to kill you last night." Eileen looked at me and tried to scowl. "Of course, nobody in this place tells me anything. You had a wild-West shoot-out last night, but I wouldn't know about it until I read tonight's paper if the reporters hadn't called."

"It wasn't much. He was a lousy shot."

"Tomorrow it might be a good shot."

"Don't worry," I said. "If it's ever me instead of him, the authorities will be waking you up to tell you."

She shook her head, and all of a sudden tears were in her eyes. "That's right. Be tough. Don't let your secretary hear any bad news. You think I don't know when there's trouble? I can tell the second things go bad. You clam up. You say nothing and make little jokes. Ha, ha."

I handed her my cup. "Here, you need this more than I do. I'm all right. Really I am. There're some other people I'm not so sure about, that's all. Come on, take a swig. It's good brandy."

"I know that," she answered, and took a quick drink. "I bought it in a very exclusive, special kind of liquor store."

"How much?"

She shook her head. "It's on me."

"You know something? You're as cockeyed a secretary as I am a detective."

She gave me a look, a sudden warm, melting look. Then she handed back the cup. "And that's not all," she said, stiffening her back and becoming efficient again. "You got another call. There's somebody who wants you to get in touch with him." She shook her head. "I shouldn't say this, Simon; I'm only your secretary. What the hell, I'm going to say it anyway. This man is dangerous.'' She leaned close. ''It may mean a lot of money, but I can tell it by the sound of his voice. He's very dangerous.''

''Who is it?''

''I can't warn you not to call him. I can only say, be careful!''

''I'll be careful,'' I assured her. ''But get him on the line. Who is it?''

''His name,'' she told me, ''is Archie Fallon. He says you know him. But you shouldn't.''

ARCHIE FALLON'S VOICE was a purr—about as reassuring as a ticking package. "Kaye?" Archie's voice said, and when I acknowledged, he continued the smooth purr, but only for about four beats. Then the hate sneaked in. "I'm telling you, you'd better goddamn well know I'm not doing this for you. You'd better goddamn well realize I wouldn't do this for anyone in the world but Doria. You get me?"

I said, "I believe you."

"So I'm gonna tell you something. You wantta listen, okay. You don't wantta listen, that's it. Doria becomes your problem. You get me?"

"I'm listening," I said.

"All right," he announced harshly. "You told me this morning about Doria's problem. You said you want to know about the protection racket in this town. That right?"

"That's right."

"I told you I didn't know nothing about it!"

"You did."

"Well, I've been doing some investigating. You wantta listen?"

"You bet I do." I was leading him on, trying to find out if he was leading me on.

He laid it on me without preamble. "I don't know who heads the racket, but there *is* one. You were right about that. Now listen to this. I wouldn't tell you this for anything in the world, but it might help Doria. So you listen. You got me?"

"I got you."

"I've got a name for you. I don't know if this guy is the head of the racket or not. If he isn't, he's high up. That's the most I can find out."

My pulses were tingling. I wouldn't have believed Archie Fallon could ever make me want to do more than throw up, but he had me hanging on his every word. "All right," I said, "what've you got?"

"There's a guy named Benny Wyckoff," Archie said.

I should have known. That did me as much good as my next-door neighbors birthing quintuplets. "Yeah?"

"You know the name?"

"I think I've heard it, but I don't know the connection. You say it's the protection racket?"

"He's in it. I don't know how high up. But he's somebody who might be able to help you."

"Yeah, all I have to do is ask."

Fallon's voice got sharp. "You're supposed to be such a hotshot detective! Can't you do something for yourself?"

You have to know Archie to love him. "Thanks

a lot," I said, keeping the sarcasm level moderate. "You're telling me there's a man named Benny Wyckoff who either heads the protection racket in this city or knows the guy who does. Is that your message?"

"Yeah, and if you want to say thank-you, I don't mind."

"I don't mind, either. But what am I supposed to do with this information?"

"I thought you were a detective. I thought all you'd need was a lead."

"Sure you did. What're you setting, a trap?"

Fallon snapped at me. "I didn't have to call you, and you don't have to do anything with the information. I'm telling you there's a guy—"

"Named Benny Wyckoff who knows who's who. You aren't telling me a damned thing. I could tell you Pancho Villa is Secretary of the Treasury. Would you believe me?"

"I'll give you more than that. Benny Wyckoff lives in the Parkview Plaza."

"Along with about fifty bodyguards, right?"

"Oh, you're scared of his security measures?" The scorn in his voice dared me to make a frontal assault.

"You guessed it."

He regrouped for a moment and tried again. "You want to see him without a lot of people around?"

"Now you're getting the idea."

He doled out another tidbit of information. "Benny's got a girl friend."

My ears picked up. "And?" I asked, sounding very casual.

"He's got her stashed in a place of her own."

"So?"

Archie's voice got sharp. He didn't like dumbbells. "So he goes to see this girl. Whaddaya think? So if you want to see him privatelike, this might be the place."

"What's the name of the girl?"

Archie said without hesitation, "Lizabeth Lynch." Then without my even asking, he added, "She lives at the Kenilworth."

If that was really her address, that was one thing. But if I knew Archie, it was more likely a trap.

I thanked him kindly and hung up. It was worth checking out, but I expected it would ring about as true as a wooden nickel on blotting paper.

THE KENILWORTH turned out to be in the redevelopment part of town and was one of those brand-new modern concrete-and-glass confections in which every tenant has a balcony and can hear all the toilets flush.

I drove around the block twice, parked and moved in for a closer look. Then I walked through the entry, gave the doorman my Henry Marvin moniker and asked to see Lizabeth Lynch.

Archie had given me straight dope. The doorman didn't blink at the name. He put in a call to

Miss Lynch from the switchboard, and next I knew, I'd been given a green light.

It was a little too pat for my taste. Archie doesn't play that kind of a game. Doria must have got to him the way nobody else had—except Moira Stevenson (Damn it, I hadn't thought of her in years. Now she'd been on my mind off and on ever since he showed me her picture.) Or he was setting me up for a killing further down the line.

I rode the elevator four floors, did two turns and rang the bell for 4G, but I had my hand on my gun while I waited.

Lizabeth opened the door clad in a pink pantsuit, no makeup, and her hair in curlers, and she wasn't at all glad to see me. "What are you doing here?" she said, looking up and down the hall, pulling me inside and closing the door. "How did you find me?"

I could relax now. She wasn't bait in one of Archie's traps. "Let me see," I said. "I find you wearing a pink pantsuit, curlers—"

"I'm serious!" She was more than serious. She was frightened. "Nobody's supposed to know where I live. Nobody but Benny. But you found out!"

I nodded and thought about it. "Maybe I was supposed to."

"What's that mean?"

"I don't know. But since I'm here, are you all right? What's happened since last night?"

"Nothing. Nothing's happened. Everything's

all right. I don't need you. You've got to get out of here."

"You haven't heard from Benny?"

She was edgy and hovered around the doorknob, willing me out. "No. No. Everything's all right."

I frowned and didn't move. "He hasn't even tried to find out if you were kidnapped, if you got home?"

"He did call. Yes, yes, he did. He called just a half hour ago. He's on his way over." She put hands on my arm, pressuring me. "Now do you see? You've got to go."

"What does he want to see you about?"

Her laugh had a note of hysteria in it. "My God, what do you *think* he wants to see me about? Will you get out? I've got to get ready." She stared at me as her first thought came back. "Say, how the hell *did* you find me? I've got to know!"

I shook my head. "You tell how you do a trick and you can't do it anymore."

She pushed me harder. "Get out. You've got to get out."

I wouldn't budge. "Oh, no. Benny's the reason I'm here. I want to see him."

She shuddered in terror. "No! Oh, my God! He'd think I betrayed him! He'd kill me! He'd really *kill* me!"

She was right about that, and it gave me pause. What kind of a spot would I put her in? If I strong-armed her and lay in wait for Benny, I'd have to be prepared to handle not only Benny but whatever minions paved the way or followed in his wake. And if I failed it would be curtains for Lizabeth, a nice blond doll who should have known better and was starting to realize it.

The temptation was strong to brush her aside and go for the jugular, let the chips fall where they may. The trouble was, I'd done that with Mom and Pop Rafe, and what had that earned anyone but grief? I didn't need anything more on my conscience.

"Okay," I said, "but don't be too sure he wants what you think he wants."

She smoothed her hands over her breasts. "Don't worry," she said. "No matter what's on his mind, I'll change it."

"Sure," I said, "and I wish you luck."

Sadness crossed her face. "I didn't really mean it like that," she said. "We talked about other things last night. But you know what I'm like. I'm not bright and witty and good company. I can't type, I can't act, I can't sing. I've got only one thing in the world going for me. I've known that since I was twelve. I've got to make it last as long as I can and take me as far as it can, because when it goes, I go."

It was a lonely world she lived in. I said, "You've got one other thing. It's not much, but don't forget it."

"What?"

"That phone number I gave you. If you're in trouble, use it."

"You really mean that, don't you?"

I nodded and let her see me out the door.

So THERE I WAS in no-man's-land, between Lizabeth's cage and Benny's approach. The hall wasn't anyplace to meet him. I didn't know how many henchmen would be on lead. If I couldn't ambush him in Lizabeth's bedroom, what was the next best thing? I thought about all those balconies, one to a suite, that offered city fumes, reconstruction views and double the rent.

Although I didn't like thinking about them, the alternatives were even worse. Not only did I need to see Benny for personal reasons, but I couldn't walk off and leave Lizabeth to the purpose of his visit. Lizabeth thought she could tame him, but Benny called the shots and I had the feeling this would be a shot Lizabeth didn't know was in his armory when she took her vows.

So what the hell was there to do but climb the fire stairs to the roof and look over the parapet. I was eight floors up, and Lizabeth's balcony was four floors down. I wished it were only one.

I took a breath, went over the edge and down the support pole, like shinnying down the trunk of a tree, and got to the seventh-floor balcony. It sounds easy, and it really wasn't all that hard—except for being eight floors up. It was a little different from going down a ten-foot tree when you're ten years old and your bones are still rubber.

Without going into the hairy details, suffice it

to say I managed this uneasy method of descent to Lizabeth's balcony in a reasonably short time and with no more than a minimum of gray hairs. Then I was there on the narrow platform with sliding glass doors and draw curtains blocking my way. I tested the doors and they were locked. Trust the Lizabeth Lynches of the world. She's a gangster's moll, which doesn't win marks for modesty, but she draws curtains over windows no one can see through and locks doors no one can get to unless they're fools like me. Sometimes you wonder what makes people tick.

Inside the phone rang. When it ding-a-linged the second time, I knocked out a chunk of glass near the knob with the butt of my gun. The timing was right: Lizabeth never heard a thing. When I reached in to turn the curtain-hidden knob, her uneasily cheerful voice was telling Benny Wyckoff to come on up.

20

BY THE TIME Lizabeth was through giving Benny the okay I was inside her glass door and behind the protective curtain. It was one of those lucky deals, like breaking the bank at Monte Carlo or walking away from a totaled car without a scratch.

Lizabeth disappeared from the scene, back to the bedroom to groom herself—get the curlers out of her hair, get all that pasty gunk back on her face. And there I was hidden behind the draw curtains, peeking through the gap, my gun in my hand, ready for anything. It was a fortune teller's dream.

Then came the buzz of the door button, and into my range came Lizabeth, still wearing the pantsuit but looking quite different. The blond hair was lacquered in place, the face mask of makeup had been heavily applied, and she wore the phoniest smile of welcome since Fay Wray said hello to King Kong.

It wasn't Benny who came through the door.

It was a man with a gun, and he shoved it into

Lizabeth's stomach, making her grunt instead of scream.

A little-girl-lost look came over her face. She'd thought she was in control. She could handle the likes of Benny Wyckoff: show him her breasts and he'd be taffy candy. So much for her one-eyed view of the world. Children shouldn't go near the water until they learn to swim.

The gorilla didn't just back Lizabeth up by ramming her with the gun, he whacked her across the face and sent her against the wall. She slumped to the floor, but he caught her by the top of her pantsuit, yanked her up and whipped her cheek with the muzzle of the gun.

There are times when my heart rules my head. This was one of them, and before he could hit her again, I was out from behind the curtains with my gun pointed and a rasp in my voice like nails down a blackboard.

He stopped and held up his hands even before he turned. It wasn't what I said—I don't remember what I said—and it wasn't the gun, because he hadn't even seen it yet. So it must have been my voice. I could barely keep my finger from pulling the trigger just as hard and fast as it could, and I think that was what he heard. Because not only were his hands high above his head, but his face, when it swung my way, was the color of lime rickey.

"You're cute," I said, moving in on him. "Why don't you do something, say something, so I can kill you?"

He was steady, let me tell you. Not so much as a muscle twitched.

I grabbed the gun out of his hand, and he let it go as if it were hot. I cracked the side of his head with it. Blood flowed, but he didn't flinch. I could have broken all his teeth and he'd have grinned. Just what I'd have done with him next, I don't know. I wasn't thinking or planning. I was so wrapped up in rage that I didn't see or hear a thing until Lizabeth screamed, "Look out!"

By then it was too late. Something crashed on my skull. I saw a thousand colored lights and, after that, blackness.

THE FIRST THING I KNEW was that my cheek was against the carpet and my head throbbed as if the village smithy were hammering horseshoes on it. I opened my eyes and saw feet. I closed them and heard voices: men's voices. One of the voices said, "He blinked," and then a shoe rammed into my side. "Okay, Sleeping Beauty," the voice went on, "get up. Nap time's over."

The foot prodded me, and when my reactions weren't instant, the guy gave me the point of the shoe as if he were practicing dropkicks.

I grunted and obeyed orders. A couple more of those and I wouldn't have any ribs left. I propped myself on one arm and shook my head numbly, keeping my eyes on the carpet. I didn't know who was where or how many, and I didn't want to appear curious.

"Well, well, Sonny Boy's awake," the harsh

voice said, and the same shoe came at the side of my head. I rolled with the blow so that while the side of the sole stung like a whip, I stayed conscious.

I lay still for a couple of seconds, regrouping, and sounding from a distance, Benny Wyckoff's laconic voice said, "Don't put him back to sleep again."

"He pulled a gun on me," the harsh voice said. That made him the punk who'd pistol-whipped Lizabeth, and all the guts my gun had drained out of him had been spooned back in. He was Macho Peachy again, going to teach me a lesson.

Benny's command stopped him from doing me further damage. "Leave him be," Benny said. "I don't want any more bruises on him."

I was glad to have Macho Peachy stop, but I wasn't happy about the reason. If Benny wanted to keep my bruise level down, it meant he desired me for display purposes. I'd rather have been kicked.

But the Macho Kid held off, and I was allowed to pull myself to a sitting position, shake my splitting head and see as much as I could without seeming to gawk. Macho had his gun back, the one I'd taken away from him. He was standing in the middle of the room, gripping it as if it'd been wired to his hand.

Benny was on one side of me, at ease in the softest chair in the room, his legs stretched out. He was wearing that bored-with-it-all expression that means the trolley car has reached the end of the line.

Lizabeth was opposite him, in a small chair by the bedroom door.

There was blood on her pantsuit and blood on her face. Her makeup didn't look too good, either, but she didn't notice. All she did was stare at Benny, lick her lips and wait to see when she'd get hit, and how mortally.

There was one other man in the room. He was behind me where I could only feel him. This would be the guy who'd sapped me. He'd been out in the hall letting Macho Man rough up Lizabeth, and when I horned in he bombed me out. It was as simple as that.

And Benny? He'd have been sitting in his car waiting for the all clear.

I slowly shifted myself to face Benny. He was the high honcho waiting to be recognized. The other man moved when I did, so I still couldn't see him. Maybe I wasn't supposed to know he was there.

Benny looked down at me pityingly. "Simon Kaye," he said. "Private detective. You stick your fingers in a lot of pies. Don't you know any better?"

He really expected an answer. He was waiting for me to say something. I said, "I'll turn over a new leaf tomorrow."

He let that pass. "Do you realize," he said, as if in reprimand, "that you killed one of my men, you critically injured another and you ran off with my girl?"

"I kidnapped her," I said, trying to smooth

her path. "But I didn't hurt her." I gestured. "She's as good as new."

That, I realized as I took a look at her, didn't promote my cause. She looked like last year's Christmas card.

"You don't have to explain," Benny said. "I can read and write." He raised his eyes to the man who stood behind me. "Strip 'em," he said. "Put 'em in bed together. It's a love-nest murder-suicide. Got it?" He pointed a finger my way. "And use *his* gun."

Benny, the entrepreneur, heaved himself to his feet and buttoned his overcoat.

I said, "You don't think you're going to make the cops believe that, do you?"

"I don't care what the cops believe."

"They're going to find out you pay the rent on this apartment. They're going to be knocking at your door."

"At my lawyer's door," Benny corrected. "But don't you worry about me. That's my problem. Worry about yourself." He flicked a finger at the lieutenant to my rear, went out the door and closed it quietly behind him.

IT WAS A FUNNY THING! Through all of this my head was splitting, so it took a conscious effort to keep from holding it in my hands and rocking with the pain. But the moment the latch clicked behind Benny, my head stopped hurting. I didn't feel a thing anymore. I guess when death walks in the door, headaches fly out the window.

I got my first look at the guy who'd given me the headache when Benny's retreat put him in charge. He gave me his own boot in the ribs and said with a sneer, "On your feet, punk, or I'll cave in your sides. I don't give a damn if you show bruises."

I got up and turned around. He was stout, with pig eyes and a red mustache. His mouth was a perpetual leer. He pointed a gun with a silencer on it, and my own gun bulged his pocket. In his left hand he hefted the sap he'd hit me with, and you could see how he wanted to do it again.

But he had even more fun things on his mind, and when I sat where he told me to sit, he turned his attention to the playmate who really interested him; the stricken and silent Lizabeth sitting in the straight chair opposite.

"Whaddaya know," he said to his friend for our benefit. "Ya hear what Benny said?"

The dumb Macho nodded.

The lieutenant jerked a finger at her and me to transmit his message. "Benny said we strip the two of 'em. Ya got that?" He chuckled mirthlessly. "Then we put 'em in bed!" He gestured at the bedroom door. "And then we make it look like a lovers' quarrel!" He stamped a foot and laughed so hard he retched.

Macho Man nodded. "Yeah, I know."

Benny's lieutenant took command again. He pointed his gun at Lizabeth. "You," he ordered. "On your feet."

Lizabeth came slowly alive. She looked to me

for a sign. I nodded. Her makeup was smeared, there was blood in her hair, on her face and on her jacket, but she rose with a toss of her head.

The lieutenant leered at her and waved his gun. "Strip," he said.

She did nothing.

His face hardened. "Did you hear what your boss said?" He waved his gun. "He said, you strip."

There was a maniacal light in the guy's eye that said he had a very short fuse. Lizabeth looked at me and I nodded again.

Slowly she unbuttoned the stained top of her pantsuit. She opened it, revealing a white bra, and, when I nodded, slipped it off her shoulders and dropped it onto the chair beside her. She did it artfully, sensually, if you will, and she wasn't even trying. She was petrified, a puppet on a string with me the puppeteer. She would only do what I told her to do, and I had to make her do whatever they wanted because to balk meant instant death. Death had to be postponed as long as possible.

"Come on, come on," the lieutenant said, gesturing impatiently with his gun. I wished she weren't so damned attractive, and that she didn't undress so sensually, but I had to nod to her to continue.

She carefully and slowly undid the hook and zipper and slipped down her pants. If she'd only do it fast, or turn her back, or be awkward, or cry a lot, I could have stood it better. But she was as sexy as a stripteaser; and this slob lieutenant beside me, aiming his gun unwaveringly the whole time, was drooling spittle down his chin. His mind was telling him, if you gotta kill, there's no harm in having some fun along the way.

She kicked her pants to one side and stood before us all in panties and bra and sandals.

"Stop stalling," the slob said when she paused.

Her mouth tightened, and she took another cue from me, kicked off her sandals and unhooked her bra. She looked at me desperately for another sign, but all I could do was nod to go ahead. We were both going to be stripped and shot unless, somewhere along the line, something gave. So far their chain of events had no weak links.

Lizabeth removed the bra and flung it across the room. It was the only expression of resentment she could get away with.

Then there was nothing left but her pants. She pulled those down to her ankles and kicked them aside. The slob was drooling from the mouth, and the Macho Kid was goggle-eyed. I was measuring distances, but it was no go. Lizabeth had charms to enthrall, and they were enthralled, but they were also careful to protect their flanks.

"Yeah," breathed the slob, unable to keep his eyes off her.

Macho Man had better control. "Okay," he said to her, waving his own gun. "Into the bedroom." He turned to me, his gun muzzle swinging. "You're next. On your feet. Strip."

Lizabeth was eager to escape. When I rose, she turned to dart inside.

The slob had other ideas. "Stop!" he said, making her turn in the doorway. Macho Man was startled at the countermanding of orders by his superior, and looked to him nervously for instructions.

The slob gave out with them. "You stay out here with him," he said, and pointed at me. "Make him strip! I'll mind the girl!" He started toward her. "Give me half an hour."

"But she doesn't need minding," Macho Man said. "Besides, I can have this one stripped in two minutes. We can be out of here in five."

The slob called Macho Man some four-letter names and told him half an hour. Then he brushed by, shoved the naked lovely girl into the bedroom and slammed the door.

Enlightenment dawned on the face of Macho Man. He'd been so busy proving he was a man among men he forgot there were two sexes to conquer. Now he gulped and turned red and backed off a couple of steps while he adjusted to the idea of taking liberties with Benny's orders.

It was only for a moment. Then he was aiming his gun and telling me to take off my clothes, I was going to be next.

I kicked off my shoes. There was silence behind the closed door. Macho Man kept darting glances at it. He was as uneasy as I. Pistol-whipping a girl was easy. What his buddy was doing shook him up. It was as if he believed women were born to be punished but not ravished.

I took my pants off and held them by the cuffs. I shook and straightened them, waiting.

Lizabeth let out a cry, and Macho's eyes darted. I swung the pants and leaped.

He tried to bring the gun around, but the pants tangled his arm. He was wrestling with them and cursing when my karate chop broke his neck.

I pulled the gun from his limp hand and kicked open the bedroom door. The slob had Lizabeth down on the bed. His pants were off and he was struggling with her when the sound of the bursting door told him he had company. He spun half off the bed thinking it was his pal, and angry oaths were still coming out of his mouth when he discovered his mistake. Then his jaw hung and his arms sagged. That's what I wanted to see, the son of a bitch.

I put two bullets through his face, one after the other, and only pulling the trigger on Benny would have given me more pleasure. He skidded across the throw rug till what was left of his head hit the baseboard. I threw the gun at him and turned to Lizabeth. "Don't look at him," I said. "Put on a dress and a pair of shoes. Grab your purse and all your valuables, because you aren't coming back."

I went through the dead man's pockets while she went through the closet, saying, "I didn't know it would be like this!"

I recovered my gun, went out to put my pants

and shoes back on, and when she had her purse and jewel box and a small overnight bag, I led her past the other body and out the door. She blinked at the second corpse and said, "Oh, God, both of them?"

"Don't cry," I told her, "count your blessings."

I took her down in the elevator, out to my car and over to my condo, and nobody said boo. I don't know what you have to do in that place to make the neighbors complain.

Up till I got Lizabeth through the door of my bachelor pad, I'd forgotten she wasn't the only one the hoods had been beating up on. The adrenaline had been pumping so fast I'd forgotten I had a headache, I'd forgotten I'd been slugged. Now that I had her rescued, the reaction set in; and no sooner had I got her through the foyer and into the step-down living room than I keeled over and all batteries went dead.

I was like that for two minutes, she told me later, and she spent the time loosening my tie, feeling my pulse, washing my face and bathing the bloody parts of my hair. Because my pulse was strong she didn't phone for an ambulance, but she was beginning to get the urge by the time I blinked my eyes and started staring at the ceiling.

Then she kissed me and thanked me for saving her and asked how I felt. What had waked me wasn't her ministrations, but the granddaddy of all headaches, and the first thing I did was groan and the second was to mumble that her kiss wasn't at fault. I told her where the aspirin was, and after three of those and twenty minutes to take effect, I was improved enough to let her help me to bed.

She maneuvered me out of my clothes and into my pajamas and worried about a concussion. Then she worried because I put my gun under my pillow. After that she worried because I told her it helped me sleep.

"You think somebody's going to come here for us?"

I didn't lie to her. "They may. Benny's not going to be very happy."

"But he's—" She studied me. "He called you a private detective. He said your name is Simon Kaye."

"That's right."

"Then the Henry Marvin business—"

"It was supposed to fool him. It didn't."

"You're investigating him?"

"Some of the things he's into."

She put her hands to her face. "How did I get into this mess? Why did I think it was glamorous to have diamonds and furs and be a big man's girl? Why didn't I listen to my mother? Why couldn't there have been a boy next door?"

I lay back and closed my eyes. The pain wasn't as bad that way. "What're you going to do when you leave here?"

She came half off the bed in alarm. "When do I have to leave here?"

"As soon as you know what you're going to do."

She took my hand in hers. "Could I stay? I can cook and sew, I really can. And I'm very good in bed. I'll prove it if you want, just as soon as your headache's gone."

"I'm not the boy next door," I said.

"Well, I wasn't really proposing," she answered sadly. "I guess I was seducing."

"Why don't you *go* back home?"

"You can't go back home. Somebody important said that. You can't ever go back."

"You can't turn back the clock, is what he meant. He didn't say you can't start over."

"God, I've spent all this time getting this far! What're you talking about?"

"I'm saying, maybe there's more to you than just your body."

"I'd like to know what it is."

I let the subject drop. Something would have to be done with her in time. Right then I needed to sleep.

I GOT ENOUGH SLEEP that it was dark when I woke up. Lizabeth did the waking. She was beside me in the bed and she stirred. I had my gun in my hand before I knew who she was. "What the hell!"

It was dim in the bedroom, but light enough to see. What she saw was the gun, and it frightened her. She'd seen what guns could do. "No, please," she said, "it's only me."

She was half out of the covers now, and she didn't have any clothes on.

I said, "What the hell!" again.

"Please, I was lonely," she said. "I didn't mean anything. I just wanted to snuggle a little and keep warm. And you were—you weren't going to know."

"Until you woke me up!" I was angry.

"I didn't mean to wake you up," she whispered. "I heard something outside. I think I did."

Never mind the anger. I was out of that bed and down the stairs in the dark, gun in front of me like a Trojan's shield. There came a pounding on the front door that only the police know how to do.

What the hell, they weren't unexpected.

I thrust my gun under the living-room couch, turned on lights and let in the law-enforcement agencies. They consisted of Brutus May, captain of detectives, and Stanley Jerome, a brutalizing former aide.

"I suppose this is not a pleasure call," I said.

May didn't answer. He strode through the foyer into the kitchen, then looked down into the living room. Jerome followed with the rolling walk and hanging arms that were supposed to make you think he swung from trees.

May descended into the living room, gazed around and lifted a cushion off the couch.

I said, "Do you have a search warrant, or did you only come to talk?"

May let the cushion down and turned around. He was only seeing how far he could go. "What've you been doing today?" he asked.

"Working."

He came back up to the kitchen alongside Jerome. "Doing what?"

"Private investigations. My occupation."

"Whereabouts?"

"*Private* is the operative word."

He didn't like that. The police, when they see me on business, usually don't. Cops can be nice and friendly until you ask them what they're up to. Then the freeze sets in. I'm the same way. I learned it when I was a cop. He leaned against the doorpost. "You know a guy named Benny Wyckoff?"

"I know who he is."

"You know he pays the rent on a pad at the Kenilworth?"

"That's not where he lives."

"I didn't say he did. I said he pays the rent there."

"For a girl?"

"That's a fair assumption."

"How does that involve me?"

"Why don't you take a guess?"

"If you think I was two-timing him with her, you've got to be crazy. I'm not that desperate for a woman."

"You mean you think you'd be in trouble if you tried?"

"I don't think he'd take kindly to such an arrangement."

"He might send some of his boys after you, huh?"

"I wouldn't be surprised."

"Like that assassin last night?"

"He came from Benny?"

"What do you think?"

"Come off it. I haven't been playing with Benny's girls. I told you, I've got better ways of keeping my health."

May still gave me the gimlet look, and Jerome was fixing me with that phony hard-eyed stare boxers use on each other when the ref is giving them his instructions. I laughed. "All right, what happened at the Kenilworth, when did it happen, and why do you think I'm involved? And while you're at it, tell me about the girl. Is she pointing her finger at me, and if she is, why do you believe her?"

Jerome moved closer and said out of the side of his mouth, "We don't answer questions, bud, we *ask* them."

I jerked a thumb at him and said to May, "You let him walk around without a leash?"

Jerome pulled a fist back, and May caught it. "You know better than that," he told the big guy quietly. To me he said, "There was a shooting in that apartment this afternoon, and we got a tip you were in on it."

"Who from, Benny?"

"It's an anonymous tip. We're just checking it out."

"Sure," I said. "Anonymous. By the way, how *is* Benny? Is he still living at the Parkview Plaza?"

"You've been there? I thought you said you hardly—"

"He hires me to watch the silver on his nights out."

"And what about his girl friend? Does he hire you to watch out for her, too?"

"Give me her name and her measurements and I'll check the file."

Jerome said impatiently, "Christ, why don't you run him in and be done with it? We can be here all night."

I turned to him. "You got something to arrest me for, Stanley?"

"Jesus," Stanley said to May, "he killed two people. You know it and he knows it. Why doncha read him his rights, let him call his lawyer and throw him in the slammer?"

May said, "Why don't you shut up?" He turned to me. "All right, you heard him. What do you know about the scene?"

I put a finger to my head. "Let me see if I can figure it out. It's the girl friend who lives in the Kenilworth. Two people were killed there this afternoon. Benny wasn't one, obviously. So it would be the girl and—let me guess—a man! They were in the hay together, and someone interrupted them. And an anonymous tip—from Benny, of course—says I'm the one." I looked from one to the other. "How close am I?"

May said, "Let's put it this way. What were you doing at five o'clock this afternoon?"

"You mean, after office hours?"

"That's right. After office hours. From five o'clock till now."

"Let's say I came home and had supper, all right?"

"And got into your pajamas and went to bed because you were plumb tuckered out."

"Sometimes I go to bed for other reasons."

May jerked a thumb at the stairs. "You willing to let me take a look around up there?"

"Not without a search warrant."

"Who is she, Simon?"

"A gentleman doesn't kiss and tell. He doesn't even concede he kisses."

Jerome said, "Let me bust him one, boss. Just one."

May ignored him. "Let me guess," he said. "She's blond, about this tall and shaped like this." He molded her with his hands. "And she answers to the name of Lizabeth Lynch. Am I warm?"

"Like an igloo."

"Well, now," May said musingly, "if I left Stanley on guard and went for a search warrant, which would take about three-quarters of an hour, would you want to lay a little bet on what we find up there?"

We were interrupted by a sound at the stairs. It was Lizabeth coming down. Except that she was wearing my bathrobe, her eyebrows were black, she had a bath towel around her head as if she'd just taken a shampoo, and showing beneath the towel were the edges of black curls. "Honey," she said in Atlanta dialect, "ah jes' hope ah didn't keep you waiting—" Then she said, clutching the robe around her throat, "Mercy me, ah din' know you was entertainin'. It's all right, gennemen. Ah'm his sister. Ah'm sure he's tole you all about li'l old me." And back up the stairs she bolted.

I gestured after her with my thumb and said, "She's my sister."

Jerome was gawking and May was muttering. He shoved Jerome toward the door. "Get moving," he said. "Stop wasting my time."

I followed them out and said, "When you see Benny, give him my love."

BACK IN THE BEDROOM, Lizabeth was as I'd seen her, black eyebrows, black ringlets and all. "What the hell did you do?" I said, laughing and pulling the bath towel away from her head. Blond hair spilled out, and she said, "Watch it, there's shoe polish on the ends."

"And eyebrows?"

She nodded.

"And that Southern drawl?"

"I started out as an aspiring actress. Doesn't every girl? I mean, it wasn't my life's ambition to go with Benny. It just beats starving."

"And all actresses have to know how to talk Southern."

She nodded. "Not so much for the stage or the cameras, but for the producers and directors, and the third assistant cameraman's cousin." She came close up and cuddled against me. "Y'all are so big and strong, and ah'm such a frail, soft li'l thing, ah doan know what ah'd all do. See how soft and helpless ah am?" She pulled open the robe to show me.

"It works every time," I assured her, and removed the robe.

In response she removed my pajamas, and for an hour and a half we had an uninhibited ball. It only happens when the pressure's off and everything's right. And it's not all that common an occurrence. This was one of the times.

THEN, when we were lying in each other's arms, deliciously sated, sprawled and sleepy, when I was already nodding off, the phone rang.

It took three rings to bring me back to reality enough to untangle the arm that was around Lizabeth, roll over and lift the receiver.

"Hello?"

"Simon?" The voice was Doria's, and it was frantic.

I got to an elbow. "What? What's the trouble?"

"The store! They threw another bomb!"

I sat on the edge of the bed. "Are you all right? Did anybody get hurt?"

She was sobbing now. "I'm all right. But mom and pop are dead."

22

I LEFT LIZABETH SLEEPING and drove like hell to the remains of the store. The ambulance was still there and so was the crowd. It was midnight, but everybody was out, white-haired crones bent over their canes, little children playing tag. There were two police cars and a fire engine, a couple of searchlights and the carrying voices that periodically issued from the communications radios.

The inside of the store was rubble. Firemen were stepping through it, poking, lifting. One of the bodies had been removed, and they were trying to get at the other.

I hunted through the group of gapers behind a couple of police sawhorses, looking for Doria. She wasn't up front, but Archie Fallon was. We would have avoided each other, but our eyes met.

"What are you doing here?"

"You think I don't care about Doria's folks?" he said snappishly.

"How'd you hear about it?"

"The way I hear about everything that goes on in this town."

"You hear who did it?"

"That, I don't have a pipeline for. But if I find out. . . ." He let the words hang.

I went on looking for Doria and finally found her, grimy and singed, wearing somebody else's coat, sitting on front steps three doors away, tended by a couple of neighbor women.

She was dry eyed and numb, but her face was a study in pain. She said, "Hello, Simon," in a dead voice. One of the women moved her feet so I could kneel on the step below.

I didn't say I was sorry. I might as well have said I did it. Pop had assured me nothing that happened would be my fault, but I couldn't accept his absolution. To me, mom and pop were dead because I'd kept Doria from taking to the streets. That was the price extracted from me, and I didn't know why she'd still speak to me, for I knew that was a price she wouldn't have paid.

But she did speak, and all I could do was kneel at her knees and ask what happened. She was hazy. It was ten o'clock, they were closing up, she was in the back, her folks were up front, and suddenly there was a tinkle of glass from the front door and a tremendous explosion. It had blown her through the doorway into the storage room. She was bruised and battered and not seriously hurt, but what she saw when she picked herself up started her screaming. She'd clawed through the wreckage yelling to her folks and getting no answer, until other people came and pulled her away.

As soon as she'd recovered enough wit to function, she'd phoned me. Since then she'd let herself be comforted by the friends and neighbors who took her in hand.

Had she called her boyfriend?

No, she hadn't. She didn't think she could go through that scene at that moment. Maybe tomorrow.

"Did you call Archie?"

She looked at me. "Are you crazy?"

"He's here."

She said, "I don't want to see him. He didn't do anything for me when he could have. There's nothing he can do for me now."

So it was right then that Archie appeared. He'd figured that where I lighted, there Doria would be. He had a hat, probably made out of unborn doeskin, and his coat was so elegant and pure that it must have been self-cleaning.

The hat, he held in both hands. He leaned forward, putting on the step a shoe that must have been worth all the clothes in Doria's closet. "My dear," he said to her as if the rest of us were on the moon, "I came as soon as I heard." His voice was agonized. "Thank God you're safe. Is there any hope for your parents?"

"They're dead."

"Oh, my dear!" He reached for her hand, but it wasn't there. "Is there anything I can do?"

"Not anymore."

His eyes encompassed the rest of us for just a moment. Then he echoed her. "Not anymore?"

"There's nothing you can do now. It's too late."

The women and I had come back from the moon and were a little too close. He didn't choose to probe that statement.

"You know what I think of you," he said softly. Then, angrily, "This shouldn't have happened. Such things should never have happened!"

He'd lost her for good. He'd lived in the hope that she'd have to meet his terms. Now she needed nothing he could provide.

He carried it through as best he could. He calmed his voice, asked about funeral preparations, was told nothing needed his help, and was left to find his own way home.

I went back to the searchlights and watched them bring out the second body. It was under a sheet, but the arm that dangled was mom's. I felt like crying, but that doesn't even water the grass in this world. There are better ways of expending one's energy. I went back to my car and aimed it at the Parkview Plaza.

I got into the building by the service entrance with the help of my master keys, and I went up to the eighteenth floor by the service stairs. I opened the door to the carpeted hall for a peek, and all was quiet.

I went to Benny's door and listened. There wasn't a sound. No band playing, no party, no laughter and singing, no harsh voices, not even a commercial on the TV.

I tried my keys on the door very quietly. If he

had a hundred locks on the inside, I'd have to ring the bell, but first let's test for surprise.

I got a surprise. The door opened. I pushed it in a couple of inches. The place was as dark as it was silent. I slipped into the foyer and closed the door. The light of night through the windows gave the only illumination. I had my gun in my hand, and it was eerie. Where were the warnings, the flashing lights, the guards? Certainly he'd learned I hadn't been murdered. Certainly he knew I'd be coming for him, even if mom and pop hadn't been killed.

I groped my way to the bedrooms, and when I found those were empty I turned on the lights. There was nobody in the apartment. Benny had flown the coop. His suits were gone from the closets, his bureau drawers had been emptied. The shaving lotions and medications were no longer in the medicine cabinet.

Was it all because of li'l ole me? Or was someone else on his trail?

23

I TOOK FRIDAY OFF and recuperated through Saturday, tended by Lizabeth. She wasn't much good as a nurse, but she sure was a great bedfellow.

That was the trouble. She was going to have to go, and she had no place. The Kenilworth was off limits, Benny would only kill her if she could find the rock he was under, home was the place she'd slept her way out of. That meant when I gave her the heave-ho, it would be into the streets.

So be it. I mean, I can be very tough when the need arises. I could tell her, "goodbye!" and never watch her go.

The trouble with that was that I'd slept with her, and girls have a way of confusing sex with the oath of allegiance. Women are very nice. I can hardly get along without them. They are soft, cuddly and exciting. They don't beat you up, shoot at you, rob your office, bomb stores and kill people—at least, the ones I know don't. But they *do* have other ways to give you a bad time.

Saturday night I tackled the job. She was

parked in front of the color TV, the placement of her feet on the coffee table already stamping the territory with the mark of ownership. To make it stick, she was wearing a very expensive diaphanous robe that was arranged to cover nothing at all. (She'd left ninety percent of her clothes back in the Kenilworth, but she hadn't forgotten to bring that.)

I hate confrontations, especially with women. Having to go up against gun-toting hoods is bad enough, but going up against a woman is worse. I know how a man thinks. I can outmaneuver him (if I'm smart enough), but a woman. . .!

"Hello, beautiful," I said, coming down the step with a drink in my hand to keep me going.

She let me look at all the things about her that were beautiful. "Thank you. I was just watching TV."

"There's nothing like it. If I didn't have to work, I'd watch it all the time."

"It's too bad they don't show adult movies on TV. We could watch them together."

"I don't know. With you beside me in 3-D, I doubt I could concentrate on the screen."

"Now that you mention it, who needs TV?"

It was web weaving. All the time with girls it's web weaving. Eileen's the only female I can't read. The rest wave signal flags like semaphore sailors. They want your body, they want your money, they want your name, they want your job. Lizabeth wanted a meal ticket. She'd been laying the groundwork that first night, telling me her life story over too many drinks, only neither of us had realized it. I was only trying to help her, and she didn't know she needed any. Now I was saying, "Bye-bye," and she was pretending not to listen.

I sat down beside her and drank half my drink. "We have to plan your future, you and I. You can't stay here, you can't go back to your apartment. You're going to have to start a new life."

She shook her head. "Benny's after me. He'll find me and kill me."

"Benny isn't worrying about killing you. He's worrying about me killing him."

"He's got pals, he's got bodyguards. They'll get me."

"Not anymore. He's become a high-risk employer." I patted a bare knee. "You're going to have to leave here. You're going to have to find another place to go."

"Don't tell me to go home. I'd die first."

"You must have friends. There must be some people who care about you."

"Just Benny." She gave me a cold eye. "For a while I thought you did, but now you're trying to get rid of me."

"I'm a loner. Stay away from people like me. I'm not good for any girl."

"You're the best lay I ever had."

"Thanks, but sometimes other talents are called for."

"Like I say, I don't have any other talents. If I have to leave here, I guess I should go to Forty-second Street in New York City. I hear the hookers do pretty well around there."

She was still trying to make me into a meal ticket. I said, "You know, New York's a great idea. You studied acting—"

"I can't act my hat. I told you. I had the biggest tits in the class and I couldn't get Juliet in the high-school play. I mean, for Christ's sake—"

"You did a good job conning the cops the other night with that 'Ah'm his sister' routine."

She grinned. "Yeah, I wasn't bad, was I?"

"That's right. You should be thinking about Broadway, not Forty-second Street."

"Yeah." She smiled at the idea for a few seconds, then sighed. "Who'm I kidding? You have to know somebody." She smoothed her hands over her bare breasts. "Maybe burlesque? Whaddaya think?"

"You have to know somebody there, as well." I put a foot on the coffee table beside hers. "I have a small connection that might open a door. I did a job once for a Broadway actor. He couldn't pay me much, but he said if he could ever do me a favor—"

"A Broadway actor? You know a Broadway actor?" Diamonds came into Lizabeth's eyes.

"He's still a nobody," I said, "which is why he might still do me a favor. If you'd like, I could give you a letter of introduction. Maybe he could introduce you—"

"Oh, yes, yes, yes!" She was all over me with kisses, bare, bosomy and torrid.

That was the end of *that* conversation.

I PUT LIZABETH on the early train Sunday morning and went to mom's and pop's funeral in the afternoon.

Jack McGuire conducted the service in the church and out at the cemetery. Doria was there with her young man friend, and I, after introductions, stayed away. He was what she needed, not me.

Archie Fallon showed up. I wouldn't have believed he'd have the nerve; the bomb that killed mom and pop had wiped him out, as well. He paid his respects to Doria and her young man, and he didn't bare his fangs when he smiled, but he was as dead as her folks.

So the funeral went off without fireworks. Mom and pop had gone to a better world; Doria and her boyfriend would get married and live happily ever after; the sale of the store property would give the young couple a good start along the path of life; Archie Fallon would slink back into his hole; I'd go down to my office on Monday ready to tackle a new case load with new challenges. End of story: everything tidy, all problems resolved, all clouds dispelled, nothing but blue skies from now on.

Like hell! Somebody'd thrown a bomb at mom and pop, and I had to know who.

On Monday I put out feelers for Benny. There are real-estate people I know, I have friends in the police department, in the city government, and I have a lot of street contacts, particularly in the sleazy part of town where the action is. I also worked on the thesis that if Benny was gone, somebody else had to step into his shoes to keep the machinery moving. Mr. Big isn't going to stop a lucrative operation because of a lack of recruits. If the pay is great enough, there is no job, however hard, however dangerous, that will lack for candidates.

It was in vain. A week grew into two, and nothing happened.

IT WAS WEDNESDAY EVENING, three weeks after I'd started the wheels turning by taking Richie Zullo out of circulation. I was having a lonely supper in front of the TV, and wondering why I was being so damned monastic, when Jack McGuire called up. "Can you come over? There's someone to see you."

I wanted to know who, but he wouldn't tell me. He said he was on orders, but that it was important. It was, in fact, an obligation.

I didn't mind the distraction. Staying home nights racking my brains for a lead to mom's and pop's killer was the pits. I heaved myself out of my chair, did my usual check for ambushes and a dynamited car and drove over to Father McGuire's well-appointed quarters.

It was Jack, not Mrs. Honeywell, who answered the door, and when he led me into the living room, it was Lizabeth Lynch who rose from the couch. She was wearing a mink, three diamond rings, diamond earrings and enough other expensive gadgetry to finance raising the Titanic.

I looked from one to the other and I wasn't exactly pleased. I thought I'd said goodbye to the girl. "What the hell kind of a game is this?"

"Search me," Jack said. "I'm only the middleman."

"Middleman? I think you're a Jewish marriage broker."

Lizabeth was beaming. "No, really," she said, "it's not his fault, it's your fault. You gave me a phone number once, for emergencies. It turns out to be his."

Jack said blithely, "Inasmuch as I have performed my function and have a number of things to do, I'll leave you to your business." And off he went, abandoning the parlor to us.

I had uneasy feelings. I don't like encores, and this had the looks of one. "What do you mean, calling this number?" I said. "You know my name, you know my number."

"I was afraid you wouldn't let me come see you."

How do these things happen? I sighed. "All right, what's the problem?"

She shook her head and showed me her coat and her dress. "Does this look as if I have problems?"

"All right, then, what happened?"

"You know that actor you wrote the letter of introduction to?"

"Don't tell me he's made it big?"

"Oh, no. He's unemployed right now, in fact. But he knows a lot of people and introduced me around, and there's this producer—well, he's not really a producer. He gives money to producers. He's an angel. And he took a fancy to me and he bought me these clothes and he takes me places—"

I said, "And he's going to star you in his next show?"

She laughed. "Oh, no. I'm not an actress. Let's not kid ourselves. That show I put on for your cop friends, that was the high point of my career. Acting isn't what I'm doing. What I do is sit with him and watch other people act."

"He's taking over for Benny, in other words?"

"That's right, except he's much nicer than Benny. And he doesn't just want me when he's horny. He's old and he hardly ever gets horny. What he likes is just to have me with him, sit with him, talk with him, go places with him. You know, it's kind of nice. I mean, I don't kid myself. I know it's not because I'm good company, it's only because I've got big tits and bright blond hair and a sexy behind, and it makes him feel good to have people see me with him. But what the hell!" She smiled. "It's really kinda nice. Benny always kept me in hiding. Now I get to go out and go places and do things."

I frowned. "Are you trying to say that this is why you're here? You came to tell me you have a new home?"

She nodded and beamed. "You were nice to me. I was in trouble and you helped me. I just wanted to let you know it worked out, and to say thank-you."

"My pleasure."

She came into my arms and kissed the hell out of me. They were thank-you kisses, but she got pretty breathless—we both got pretty breathless—and she panted, "God, I'd love to screw you. But I can't anymore. I mean, I belong to somebody else. I hope you understand."

I said I understood.

"That actor friend of yours," she whispered, still in my arms, "thinks very highly of you. He says you helped him get rid of a crappy wife."

"Give him my regards."

"Yeah, I will." She disengaged herself and looked at a diamond-studded wristwatch. "Oh, I have to go now. He's waiting."

"Who, your angel?"

"Of course not," she said. "His chauffeur."

She wasn't kidding. Outside was a block-long limousine with a liveried driver waiting to ferry her back to New York.

It was Cinderella and the pumpkin coach, and when I handed her in and kissed her through the window, I said, "I hope you haven't forgotten your glass slipper."

"Glass?" She laughed. "Didn't you notice? They're rhinestone."

The chauffeur took off like a drag racer, and I was left with the smell of burning rubber.

I FOUND JACK behind the desk in his study, surrounded by shelves of books about God, Christ, the Pope, Good and Evil, the Bible, and the rest of what makes him tick.

"Thanks for the interlude," I said.

"A very attractive young lady, Miss Lynch," he answered, "albeit a little gaudy. Was that an S.O.S. call she was giving you?"

"It was a farewell address."

"Love 'em and leave 'em, eh?"

"It was by mutual consent."

"I take it by her trappings that she's not going to need an emergency number anymore?"

"I hope not. She's Benny Wyckoff's ex-girl friend—EX-girl friend, that is—so you never can tell."

Jack shook his head. "That doesn't sound so good. Benny's bad news from what I hear. I wouldn't play around with him, Simon."

"So you said before."

"But you tangled with him anyway?"

"I had to. I told you. He was the next rung up the ladder."

"What happened?"

"He tried to kill me. He tried to kill her, too. But it didn't work. Now he's hiding out and I'm trying to track him down."

"For vengeance, Simon?"

"Hell, no. He's my clue to Mr. Big, and Mr. Big's responsible for killing Mom and Pop Rafe."

"And instead of letting the police handle it, you feel obligated—"

"Christ," I interrupted, "stop trying to make me sound like a boy scout. Mr. Big's going to kill me, too, if he gets a chance, because he knows I'm after him. He's already tried!" I told Jack about the assassin. "So you see, I've got no choice. I've got to find him first."

Jack clasped his hands together and rubbed them against his nose. "You lead one helluva life," he finally said. "I don't know how to classify you. If you were being paid a million dollars, I could understand it. But you're not even getting expenses."

"Like hell," I said. "If I were getting a million dollars you *couldn't* understand it. It's only because I'm not even getting expenses that you know what I'm talking about."

Jack sighed. "I don't know whether you're going to go to heaven or hell, but whatever the place, you're sure going to liven it up."

"If it's hell, I'll still be gunning for Mr. Big."

Jack shook his head and stroked his nose some more. "You don't have any clue at all as to who he is?"

"Not that I can identify."

"There's no way you can track down Benny?"

"I don't know. If he rents or buys anything in town, no matter under what name, I'll find it out. Anyone checking into any hotel or motel who answers his description, I'll be told. That's as far as it goes."

Jack's eyebrows arched. "This must be costing you a fortune."

"Not a cent. I have a lot of friends in a lot of places."

"That assassin you killed. He came from Mr. Big?"

"He had to."

"Too bad he couldn't have been made to talk."

"That's not the way it's done," I said. "He wouldn't have known who Mr. Big was. He was only carrying out an assignment. His superior would supply him with a target and a prepayment. He'd go hit the target and collect the balance when the death was verified." Then I said, "Wait a second. The assassin not only had my address, he had an ID on me." I reached in my wallet and produced the clipped piece of snapshot I'd found on his body. "Look at this," I said. "Somebody gave him this likeness to go with the address."

Jack studied the picture of my head and bare shoulders, one shoulder cut off at the edge. "You look about twenty years old," he said.

"Somewhere around then."

He studied the picture some more. Then he left

the room and came back with a large, very thick photo album, which he flopped on the desk. I moved in beside him. "You think you have the rest of that picture?"

"Remember the camera I saved up for? I was the shutterbug in the gang. I must have taken ten times more pictures of you than anybody else."

"Yeah, but Mr. Big wouldn't be getting hold of any of those."

It was worth a try, though, and Jack flipped through the pages looking for anything of me with a bare torso.

Halfway through we found it, a snapshot of me standing with Moira Stevenson in our bathing suits on the city beach with the Long Island Sound at our backs. Jack and I matched it with the assassin's pic, and there was no question. The lock of hair over the forehead, the proud expression on my face. One didn't have to see my arm around the girl to know she was there. The assassin's picture had been cut from a five-by-seven enlargement of that shot.

And who would have such an enlargement? It was Jack who said it. "Archie Fallon!"

It was the same thought that had hit me—because of Moira, of course—but I struck snags. "Wait a minute," I said. "Why?"

He pointed at the girl. "Because she's in it. She'd have asked me for an enlargement. And I'd have made her one."

"Yeah, yeah, it's a good picture of her. But how would Archie come by it?"

Jack said impatiently, "From Moira's possessions, of course. After she died. It would be in her album, and Archie would inherit it."

That didn't make sense. "What're you talking about? Moira was in love with Archie, and she knew how I felt about him and how he felt about me. You're crazy if you think she'd marry Archie with pictures of *me* in her album! It's the bride-to-be burning old love letters. You don't go into marriage wearing your past."

Jack shook his head. "Take my word for it, she'd have had that picture. Archie's your man."

"I won't take your word for it. You don't know what the hell you're talking about. You ought to know Archie, and you ought to know Moira. She wouldn't do a thing like that to the man she loved, and Archie wouldn't have stood for it. The last thing he'd allow would be my picture in his house."

Jack put his face in his hands for a moment and slowly looked up with the most miserable of expressions. "Maybe you'd better sit down."

"I'm all right standing."

"So be it." He said to me, "I haven't told you this before because Moira didn't want me to. And there's something else you don't know, but now maybe you should."

That sort of thing grates. I don't like being treated like a baby, too innocent and tender to be told the truth. I had very caustic comments on my lips, but held them back. Jack was as distraught as I was, and you don't hit a man when he's hurt. "All right, what have you got to tell me?"

Jack sighed and took a deep breath. "Moira," he said slowly and carefully, "did not die in an accident as you, as Archie Fallon and as the rest of the world believe."

"How, then?"

Jack swallowed. "Suicide."

"Suicide!"

Jack nodded.

"She was only married two months."

"It was enough."

"What, why, how—"

Jack shook his head. "It's irrelevant. The other part is—and I'm really afraid to tell you this—Moira was in love with you."

"Moira?"

He nodded, and I had never seen him so miserable and uncertain.

"She married Archie."

Jack swallowed. "She didn't want to."

"But she said—I was too young—"

"You know better than that."

"And that Archie—that she was in love—"

"There were . . . pressures—forces—considerations. There are things I cannot talk about. All I can tell you is, she thought there was no other way. She wanted you, but she thought she had to marry *him*. And two months later she killed herself."

I didn't say anything. I couldn't say anything.

I'd be a long time getting to the point where I could *think* anything.

Jack closed the album. "While she was alive I had to be quiet. After she died, there was no point in speaking. Now, I don't know if it's the right thing to say what I'm saying."

I thought about the might-have-beens and pushed them away. What good does it do? I picked up the cropped photo I'd been carrying. How Archie must have hated those pictures of me that Moira had kept. He wouldn't have known she had them until she was dead, of course. She was that kind of a girl.

And now, after all these years, he had a use for such pictures. He could crop out my head and send it to an assassin to make sure the man he killed was me.

I SAID GOOD-NIGHT to Jack. He said he hoped he'd helped me and not hurt me, and I said he had. He'd given me a lead.

He wanted me to realize his theory that Archie was Mr. Big might be in error, and I assured him that was something to contemplate. I even pointed out that killing Mom and Pop Rafe ruined Archie's cause, so why would he do that?

Jack wanted me to go home and sleep on it, and I said sure.

So I got out of there, but I didn't head for the condo. If I went home and slept on it, I'd get smart in the head and scared in the stomach.

Archie was Mr. Big as sure as the stars shine. He was the "Chief" Benny Wyckoff called. He was the one who provided the assassin with the identification snapshot of me. He was the one who gave me Lizabeth's address so Benny and his men could trap and kill us both. As for killing the Rafes, that was an accident. Archie meant only to give the screw another turn and bring Doria down as in another day and age he'd brought Moira Stevenson down.

It was now or never. Time was awasting. I had a set of proper tools in the trunk of the car—that which burglars cart around in their tote bags when they take their midnight constitutionals. So it was out to what used to be the public library before TV and Archie's millions gave it a different dimension.

I parked the heap three blocks away and made the rest of the trip in the shadows. There was a wrought-iron fence surrounding the place, but it was a snap to climb with a coil of rope. The inside grounds were modest, for the old library couldn't afford a substantial tract of urban land. There were no guard dogs, no guards, no roving searchlights. It was nothing more than the quiet home of a well-to-do real-estate agent who didn't need to take more than the ordinary precautions against burglars. There would be alarms connected to the windows and doors, but that would be the whole of it. What I was counting on was that they'd overlooked the ventilation tunnel.

Basement windows peeked three feet above ground with the rest of their length looking out into air shafts. The third such shaft gave access not to a basement window but to the heavy wire screen at the outside entrance to the tunnel. Jack and I had found that out years ago.

I slipped into the pit and used a pencil flash to check the fastenings on the screen. A Phillips screwdriver would undo them all.

I laid the screen on the ground outside, then slipped into the yard-square passage. It was smaller than I remembered it, and I was not as nimble. It was slow going, and I had to blink my pencil flash periodically to find my way. Then, close to the other end, I could detect the faint glow of night-lights.

I got to the inside screen, the one that gave access to an alcove in the living room. I was prepared for the tedium of cutting my way through with wire snips, but damned if it didn't push right out! Nobody had ever replaced the holding screws Jack and I had removed. Probably nobody had even noticed they were missing.

I set the screen to one side and climbed out into the living room. I was all alone, and the silence was unreal.

The trip to Archie's office was silent and quick. Archie was being kind to me, for night-lights showed the way. The office itself was black and empty with only the glow of outside streetlights to guide me around the furniture.

I latched the door but couldn't lock it, for there was no key. Next I drew the window draperies and switched on the desk lamp. The files were in the corner beside the copying machine, and I brought the top drawer to the desk. Everything in it dealt with real estate. Nothing funny there.

The middle drawer was more of the same. I replaced it and brought out the bottom one. That bore the label Miscellaneous, which was strange. A whole drawer of miscellaneous?

The first folder was the jackpot. Right in front was a sheet of names with lists of stores against each one and the weekly collection fee in a column on the right. The uninitiated wouldn't know what it meant, but I'd been behind the scenes and knew enough of the names and enough of the sums to recognize what it was.

I made myself five copies of the sheet on the machine, then went through the rest of the folder, duplicating everything that looked good. It took only twenty minutes, but when I was through I had enough evidence on Archie Fallon to blow his kingdom to the moon. Who threw every bomb, who rented what car, did what job, spent what money, reported what result—it was all there. A meticulous man, was Archie Fallon. He kept a record of everything.

When the job was done and I was sliding the drawer back, it made a slight scraping noise. It wasn't much, but it almost covered the sound of the doorknob turning.

I jumped around, and my gun was in my hand. My reflexes work pretty fast at times like that.

The knob turned again, tentatively, and the door started to open. It was so slowly and gingerly done that I could duck over by the window and come up on the back side.

When it came wider, I yanked it out of the guy's hand and shoved my gun in his face. It was Benny, holding a gun of his own, and he almost fainted.

I hit him with the barrel of mine, took his, threw him into a chair, closed the door again and went behind the desk where I could watch both him and the door.

"So you didn't blow town," I said, and called him a few names I won't repeat. He was terror-stricken, spread all over the chair like a jellyfish. He couldn't even move. After a while his lips quivered and he got the words out.

"It's you!" he whispered.

"Yeah," I said. "You thought you left me for dead, didn't you?" I called him a few more unprintable names. "Where's your boss? Where's Archie?"

He shook his head. "I dunno." He couldn't take his eyes off my gun.

"It doesn't matter," I told him. "I've got to go now. And you're going with me."

"No," he croaked. "No please!"

"And if you're a very nice guy and want to turn state's evidence and help us send Archie to jail, you might not only get to live, you might even go free. That sound pretty good to you, you—" I had a few more names for him in my vocabulary.

I laid my gun beside his on the desk in a gesture of goodwill. "You see?" I said. "No hard feelings. I don't want to kill you. Not much, anyway. All you have to do is squeal on Archie."

He didn't move. I snapped my fingers at him. "On your feet, punk. Whether you talk or die doesn't matter. We're walking out of here and the time is now."

Then a voice behind me said, "Stick 'em up."

27

YOU THINK you're king of the hill, and something like that happens. It's like coming home from vacation and finding the bathwater running.

I didn't have to turn around to know who was behind me. And I knew there wasn't anything I could do except put up my hands. There's no place Archie would rather shoot a man than in the back, and I didn't want to tempt him.

"All right," Archie snarled at Benny. "Get the guns."

Benny came out of his chair and reached for them, a hand for each, eyeing me as if I might strike him dead. I'd walked away from so many traps that even when I was at bay he was afraid. He backed off quickly, tucking my gun in his pocket, covering me with his own.

"All right, ya creep," Archie told me. "Over by the window."

I moved obediently to the spot, keeping my hands high, and turned around. The panel behind his desk was open. It was a silent door on a spring latch that didn't look like a door. I don't know why I don't think of such things.

Both Benny and Archie had me covered, but Archie did the talking. "Now, you son of a bitch, you're gonna get what's been coming to you for more than twenty years. Breaking and entering, huh? Carrying a gun, huh? An armed robber invading a private citizen's home, huh? You know where that leaves ya, don'tcha, ya punk?"

I thought of Moira, the girl who'd taken her own life rather than stay with him. I thought of Doria, who'd have sold her body to escape him. He'd made me believe he'd stolen Moira away from me, but I realized now that he knew it wasn't so. I'd thwarted him with her as I'd thwarted him with Doria. And don't forget the little girl I'd kept him from molesting when I was seven. I'd had it coming to me for more than twenty years, he'd said. It went all the way back to her. Girls were where his ego lay, and he was going to see me dead. That message was on his face in capital letters.

"Ya know what we got here?" he said to Benny. "We got an armed robber in the house. We can put enough lead in him to sink the *Bismarck*, and the cops can't do a thing." He was starting to gloat now, telling it for my benefit. "The law's on our side."

He outlined the plot to make sure I understood. "Ya know what we do? We leave him lying dead on the floor and call the cops. Ya get what I mean? It's our civic duty."

Benny nodded like a puppet. He wouldn't believe it until I was lying dead on the floor and the cops were patting them on the back.

I put in an oar, not because I had anything to say, but because if you give the enemy free rein you're already dead. "Why the hell did you kill Doria's folks?" I said with proper exasperation. "She would've married you in the end if you'd let well enough alone."

That reminded Archie that he could entertain me a little longer. "One of those things," he said. "Accident, ya might call it." He grew angry at the thought. "Dumb bastards," he said of his underlings. "They were supposed to make sure the place was empty."

"So now where are you?" I persisted. "Doria's going to marry her boyfriend and you're out in no-man's-land—where you've always been."

That reminded him of another goodbye message he could give me. "I got news for you, punk! Doria ain't marrying nobody." He amplified it when I didn't catch on. "For the same reason you ain't going to the wedding. She ain't gonna live that long."

That hurt me, and he knew it. He grinned and dug the knife deeper. "You got the idea? Nobody crosses Archie Fallon. Try it and you're gonna be sorry.

"I gave her a chance. I gave her lotsa chances. She don't wanna take me up on 'em? That's her loss." His voice turned to a rasp. "She ain't ditching me for nobody else. You got that? It's me or nothing. I don't give people no choice.

That's the way I operate. That's why I'm where I am and you're where you are."

I said, "And that's why Moira Stevenson is where she is?"

That shook him, but only for a second. His hate index doubled. "Her name was Moira *Fallon*!"

"Was it—really?"

He decided he didn't want to entertain me anymore. The fun was gone. He said to Benny, "We let him talk long enough. Now we give it to him." He waved. "Hit him dead center in the heart. Let me see him bleed!"

Benny was staggered. "Me?"

"That's right. You got the honor. Blast the son of a bitch!"

"But—but—the cops—"

Archie got testy. "Didn't you hear what I said? It's our civic duty. It's on the house!"

Benny's gun trembled. "But it's *your* house."

I'd known Archie was yellow, but not *how* yellow. He didn't have the guts to shoot me head-on. Now I doubted he could even have shot me in the back. He wanted to watch me die, but from Benny's bullets.

I played on that. "Archie wants you to pull the trigger," I told Benny, "because then he'll *own* you forever."

Benny cringed and backed up a step. His gun was unsteady.

"Shoot the son of a bitch," Archie ordered.

I said to Benny, "Make Archie do it. Then you'll have him in *your* pocket."

Archie was losing command, and his voice took on an edge. "You hear what I said? Kill him!" He waved at Benny with his gun. "He took away your girl! You can't let him get away with that!"

Benny's backbone stiffened. It was the macho impulse.

I cut in fast. I said to Archie, "I took away *your* girl, too, you punk."

That slashed through the interplay like a laser. He half turned his head.

"Moira!" I snapped. "She never loved you. She was in love with me. She didn't die by accident, it was suicide. She killed herself to get away from you!"

Archie's gun came my way, and for a second I thought I'd overplayed my hand. It almost went off. But, like I say, he was yellow. And what's more, Archie never totally loses control.

Archie's gun swung back to Benny. "Shoot him, you son of a bitch," he said. "I order you. You hear me? That's an order!"

"Me?" Benny shrieked. "But it's your house—it's your girl—"

What with the ranting and raving and the uncertainty, it wasn't all that hard. I jumped Benny. One second they were fighting each other and I was part of the furniture. The next I had Benny yanked in front of me and was wrestling him for his gun.

Did I say Archie never totally loses control? Now he did! He let out a keening shriek and started shooting. I thought it was me he was after, but the bullets were going into his pal. Maybe after Benny went down he'd pump what was left into me, but right then he meant them to hit the guy they hit. Benny had screwed up his final triumph, and getting even came first.

I got hold of Benny's gun when he took the first shot. I had to support him when he caught the second, but before Archie could snap off a third, I was returning fire.

My first three bullets hit him in the chest, going up the ladder as he sagged. The last two hit him in the mouth and forehead as he fell to the floor.

Dead Benny was a drag on my arms, and I flopped him next to Archie. I retrieved my gun from his pocket, stuck his own hot weapon, with one bullet left, in his limp hand and hurried off. There had to be servants somewhere and they had to come prowling. I didn't want to be there when they did.

I played it smart. I went out the ventilation tunnel the way I'd come in. I even had the presence of mind to refit the screen in place behind me and screw the outside screen back into position so that it looked untouched. Then it was out across the grounds and back over the fence, leaving behind one of those nice little locked-room puzzles.

THE POLICE called it a shoot-out. It was listed in all the papers as open-and-shut. The records in Archie's files proved it. Benny was second in command, and the double death was regarded as the result of a power struggle.

Archie's records solved a few other cases that had been plaguing the police, such as who killed Richie Zullo and Louie the Greek; who bombed and killed the Rafes; and who was the assassin who died on my doorstep.

Unfortunately, Archie, in his meticulous, secret fashion, reported on the trap that he and Benny set for me in Lizabeth's apartment. This caused me to undergo a grilling session with the police myself. Since nobody but Lizabeth could say I was ever there, and Lizabeth had disappeared, all I had to do was stand on my rights and there wasn't anything they could stick me for.

Let's not suggest they couldn't guess what was what. They aren't dumb. But knowing and proving are two different things, a fact the police understand very well. What they can't prove they aren't going to fret about. To do so is called not being smart.

DORIA AND HER BOYFRIEND did get married despite Archie's predictions, and it would seem that everything turned out happily in the end, just like a fairy tale.

Except that Mom and Pop Rafe didn't go to the wedding. Things didn't work out happily for them. I still feel guilty about that, but at least now I can sleep nights.

Be a detective.
See if you can solve . . .

RAVEN HOUSE™ MINUTE MYSTERY #6

On the following page is Raven House MINUTE MYSTERY #6, "Miami Murder."

Every month each Raven House book will feature a MINUTE MYSTERY, a unique little puzzler designed to let *you* do the sleuthing!

U.S. (except Arizona) residents may check the answer by calling toll free **1-800-528-1404** anytime from August 16 to October 15, 1982. U.S. residents may also obtain the solution by writing anytime during or after this period to:

Raven House MINUTE MYSTERY
1440 South Priest Drive
Tempe, AZ 85281

Canadian residents, please write to the following address:

Raven House MINUTE MYSTERY
649 Ontario Street
Stratford, Ontario N5A 6W2

MIAMI MURDER
by J.A. Kripper

Inspector David Bain had arrived in Miami at noon; nine hours later he still wasn't used to the hot sun after the cold snowbound North he had come from.

Charlie Sanger's body, though, was more familiar. A New York-based Mafia man shot to death in a posh nightclub office was regrettably familiar.

Bain's old friend, Homicide Chief James Reeder, emerged from the outer office where the two girls were being held. "The bartender confirms it," he said. "Daisy walked in about five minutes after Rita. The office is soundproof, so he didn't hear anything until a few minutes later when the two of them came out screaming, each saying the other had shot Sanger."

Bain gazed around the room—at Sanger lying on the floor, the .38 near him, the handful of twenty-dollar bills on the desk, the open desk drawer containing a closed metal cashbox. "Let's go talk to them," he said.

They were both gorgeous: Rita, the club's headline singer, with black hair and skin like dark honey; and Daisy, a bright blonde with creamy skin and large blue eyes.

Daisy talked first. "When I came in Charlie had just told Rita I was going to take over her singing spot, and she was yelling at him terribly. Charlie opened the drawer, took out some bills and said, 'Take this and get lost.' And she reached over and took the gun out of the drawer and shot him!"

"Lies!" screamed Rita. "He told *you* to get lost. He was through with you. He told me he still loved me and that you'd followed him from New York."

"He begged me to come with him!" Daisy cried. "He had no more use for you—he told me so this afternoon when he took me out to catch boney fish. We were out for hours just to get away from you."

"You mean bonefish," Inspector Bain commented mildly. "Hoped to catch some myself while I was down here."

"Her whole story is fishy!" Rita said venomously. "Anyway, Charlie never liked pale, washed-out broads like... like you!"

"I was told," said Chief Reeder, "that Sanger's explanation for flying to Miami was to see how Rita was doing with the show—that he'd heard rumors."

"I think I will have time to go fishing tomorrow," said Bain. "The answer to this case is pretty obvious."

What was the clue that gave Inspector Bain the answer?